The machine gun outside slammed into life like doomsday. The wooden walls of the museum were no defense against the cigar-sized bullets that passed through them like they were paper. Glass display cases shattered in explosions of shrapnel shards. Juanita was the only one to have disobeyed Bolan, and she paid for it as a burst from the crew outside sacrificed her to the revolution.

Bolan glanced at the Beretta in his hand. They were definitely outgunned.

The weapon outside suddenly fell silent as it burned up its one-hundred-round belt. The crackle and pop of small-arms fire filled the gap as the machine-gun crew reloaded. Bolan rose to a crouch. It was time to move. "Everyone behind me!" he shouted.

The Executioner threw himself down again as he heard an unmistakable sound and the real hell-storm began.

Six-foot streaks of fire geysered through the hundred machine-gun holes perforating the museum walls. Somebody had brought along a flamethrower. They were upping the ante.

MACK BOLAN ®
The Executioner

The Executioner®
Don Pendleton's
CRISIS NATION

A GOLD EAGLE BOOK FROM
W✪RLDWIDE®

TORONTO • NEW YORK • LONDON
AMSTERDAM • PARIS • SYDNEY • HAMBURG
STOCKHOLM • ATHENS • TOKYO • MILAN
MADRID • WARSAW • BUDAPEST • AUCKLAND

Recycling programs
for this product may
not exist in your area.

First edition July 2009

ISBN-13: 978-0-373-64368-4

Special thanks and acknowledgment to
Charles Rogers for his contribution to this work.

CRISIS NATION

Printed in U.S.A.

When you are occupying a position which the enemy threatens to surround, collect all your force immediately, and menace *him* with an offensive movement.

—Napoleon I
1769–1821
Maxims of War

When my enemy thinks I am surrounded and have no way out, I will take the opportunity to make my own attack.

—Mack Bolan

THE
MACK BOLAN

LEGEND

Nothing less than a war could have fashioned the destiny of the man called Mack Bolan. Bolan earned the Executioner title in the jungle hell of Vietnam.

But this soldier also wore another name—Sergeant Mercy. He was so tagged because of the compassion he showed to wounded comrades-in-arms and Vietnamese civilians.

Mack Bolan's second tour of duty ended prematurely when he was given emergency leave to return home and bury his family, victims of the Mob. Then he declared a one-man war against the Mafia.

He confronted the Families head-on from coast to coast, and soon a hope of victory began to appear. But Bolan had broken society's every rule. That same society started gunning for this elusive warrior—to no avail.

So Bolan was offered amnesty to work within the system against terrorism. This time, as an employee of Uncle Sam, Bolan became Colonel John Phoenix. With a command center at Stony Man Farm in Virginia, he and his new allies—Able Team and Phoenix Force—waged relentless war on a new adversary: the KGB.

But when his one true love, April Rose, died at the hands of the Soviet terror machine, Bolan severed all ties with Establishment authority.

Now, after a lengthy lone-wolf struggle and much soul-searching, the Executioner has agreed to enter an "arm's-length" alliance with his government once more, reserving the right to pursue personal missions in his Everlasting War.

Laguna San José, Puerto Rico

Bolan stared at the three stripped bodies as they bobbed in the shallow water. They had bloated up from being in the salt marsh overnight. Bruises encircling the wrists and ankles showed that the two policemen and one policewoman had been bound. Brutal contusions on other parts of the police-woman's body showed that she had endured other abuses before she had been decapitated with her fellow officers. San Juan CSI had marked off the area with stakes in the silt wrapped with crime-scene tape. It was impossible to get a car down there in the mud, so a harbor patrol fan boat was making its way through the reeds. Bolan glanced up as a passenger jet roared out of Luis Muñoz Marin International Airport across the lagoon. Heat shimmered off the causeway loaded with morning traffic crossing the shallow waters. At nine o'clock in the morning, it was already ninety degrees. He glanced back at the bodies. It was getting to the point that the police no longer waited to be called. Every morning harbor patrol sent out small boats to the lagoon and more often than not they came back with bodies.

"This is bad, Señor Cooper," Inspector Noah Constante said, using Mack Bolan's cover name for this mission. He was a lanky man in a television-blue guayabera shirt and a white Kangol driving cap. He had a coppery complexion, a hooked nose and slightly almond-shaped eyes that spoke of indigenous Taino Indian blood. A pencil-thin mustache completed his look. With the Colt .45 pistol automatic tucked into the front of his tropical white silk pants, he looked like the world's most dangerous golf caddy. He lit another cigarette and tossed the old butt into the water. "Very bad."

Bolan nodded. Beheading was a favorite of method of "warning murder" with the Mexican drug gangs, and it was quickly becoming popular throughout Central and South America. To Bolan's knowledge this was the first time it had been used by political revolutionaries in the Caribbean, much less in a commonwealth of the United States.

Much less against United States military police personnel.

Puerto Rico's political status was unusual to say the least. It was currently considered an "enhanced commonwealth" of the United States and its politics were split fairly evenly along three diverging lines. There were those who wanted to maintain the status quo, and they had won referendums to keep it that way in six decades of votes on the subject. There were those who wanted Puerto Rico to become the fifty-first state of the United States and join the republic.

And there had always been a Puerto Rican independence movement.

Since the 1800s there had been those who had wanted to kick out the Spanish colonizers. When the United States had invaded the island during the Spanish-American War, there had been those who had wanted to kick out the Yanquis. That had been mollified a great deal when Harry S Truman gave all Puerto Ricans American citizenship. Still, there had always been those who sought, and sometimes fought, to gain nation-status for the Caribbean island.

The *Nationalistas* were the smallest of the three political affiliations, but they had always been the most vocal.

They had also been the one to turn to violence.

Until recently it had always been small-scale, and most of even the most ardent of those who dreamed of Puerto Rican independence shunned violence as a means to achieve it. Now, times seemed to be changing. It had begun with rumors that the U.S. military was storing nuclear weapons on the island. Political activists had begun protesting outside U.S. military bases and Puerto Rican police stations. The actions by military policemen to round them up and take them away from the bases had made news worldwide. When a protestor had been shot trying to break into Fort Buchanan, the protests had broken out into street-rioting in the capital. Tear gas and rubber bullets had been used and the rioting and looting had gotten worse.

Then people had started to die in earnest.

Anyone who opposed the closing of the bases or independence for Puerto Rico was branded a traitor. There had been a number of high-profile kidnappings, and street violence disguised as political statement had become endemic in the capital and was spilling out into the countryside. Police had become a popular target, and it was common knowledge that many Puerto Rican police were sympathetic and were not prosecuting or investigating to the best of their abilities. The United States was loath to send in armed troops or hordes of federal police. The Puerto Rican governor had called out the National Guard, and many of them were very reluctant to take action against rioters or demonstrators. Many had thrown down their weapons and joined them.

There were many in the U.S. congress and senate who believed that the U.S. should wash its hands and let the island commonwealth go. The FBI had very strong leads that Puerto Rican organized crime had a very strong hand in everything going on, but when a car bomb had gone off outside their San Juan office and two of their agents had been killed, they had been forced to admit there wasn't much they could do about it without massive reinforcement.

Puerto Rico was turning into a powder keg, and it was almost to the point of being a "retake the island or let it go" situation. The President was willing to consider Puerto Rican independence, but had stated categorically to his cabinet he would not allow the U.S. and Puerto Rico's long association to be severed by the sword of domestic terrorism rather than the ballot box.

He was unwilling to send in the 101st Airborne Division. Instead he fell back on the services of a patriotic American.

Mack Bolan had boarded a plane.

He turned and sized up the man beside him. Puerto Rico might be a commonwealth of the United States, but it was also a Caribbean island with an overwhelmingly Latin culture. Corruption among the police was endemic. Inspector Noah Constante had a reputation as an ass-kicker. He had a lot of arrests, a lot of convictions and a sleepy aura of relaxed violence about him. Bolan suspected that if Constante had been a cop on the mainland he would probably have been brought up on police brutality charges dozens of times. He was a man who got things done and specialized in homicide. That told Bolan that if Constante was corrupt, the inspector was much more likely to receive favors and bribes from local businessmen and politicians rather than criminals. That was one reason why Bolan had requested him.

"Beheadings say gangsters. I think gangsters did this," Bolan said.

"Well," Constante said, giving a very Latin shrug, "there is no reason why a man cannot be a gangster and a patriot."

Bolan tilted his head at the bodies. "You consider whoever did that a patriot?"

"Whoever did that is murdering, rapist scum." Constante's black eyes stared long and hard at the dead military policewoman's corpse. "I happened to have known Miss Corporal Carson. She was a good cop. I am afraid I cannot let this stand."

"So tell me, who's the most powerful gang in Puerto Rico?" Bolan knew the answer, but he wanted to gauge Constante.

"That's easy." The inspector shrugged again. "That would be *La Neta*, which means *the truth.* They formed in Río Piedras Prison in 1970, supposedly to stop violence between inmates and promote solidarity between the Puerto Rican gangs, but they have since, how would you say…evolved, beyond their original charter."

"What else can you tell me about them?" Bolan asked.

"They often promote themselves as a cultural group. Since their inception they have always promoted independence for the island. Like all successful prison gangs, they spread out beyond the prison walls. They have taken over many of the street gangs and established ties with others. They have always had a reputation of *silencio.*"

Bolan raised an eyebrow. "Silence?"

Constante frowned. "Not exactly." The inspector sought for a translation. "It is not the word they would use, but you would understand their reputation much more as *tranquilidad.*"

"Quiet," Bolan said.

"Yes, quiet. Make no mistake, *La Neta* is a violent street gang. Disrespect or action taken against one of their members or affiliates is seen as an attack on all members, and they will violently defend their turf. However, they have established the unusual tactic of not drawing attention to themselves, and when they do, it is as a patriotic organization—Puerto Rico for Puerto Ricans. Often they put money into their local barrios, in community projects. They will provide beer and food at fiestas and march in parades wrapped in the Puerto Rican flags. They let other gangs draw attention to themselves as gangsters, they let others establish reputations for violence and killings, for being bad men, and when the inevitable crackdown comes? *La Neta* is waiting, in *silencio*, to move in and take over their turf or swallow up their organization."

Bolan eyed the inspector shrewdly. "What about ties to political groups?"

"As I have said, *señor*, *La Neta* is strongly patriotic. They have long associated themselves with the *Los Macheteros* revolutionary group."

Bolan had read a dossier on "The Machete Men." For years they had been on the violent, extremist end of the independence movement. Bolan surveyed the headless corpses. "That look like machete work to you?"

"Indeed." Constante sighed. "However, I must say that is a tenuous, indeed, metaphoric lead at best."

The inspector had a bit of the poet about him. Bolan found himself liking the man but not immediately trusting him. "Like I said, this looks like gangster work, parading as politics, and that's where I'm going to start my way up the food chain."

"You know much about gangsters, then?"

Bolan played a card and posed a question of his own. "Tell me, Inspector, did you ever see the movie *The Untouchables?*"

"'They pull a knife, you pull a gun. He sends one of yours to the hospital, you send one of his to the morgue.'" Constante quoted. His teeth were neither particularly even nor straight, but they flashed blindingly white out of his face.

"And there endeth the lesson," Bolan concluded. "You in?"

"Oh, well, how may I be of assistance to…" He gazed at Bolan in open, smiling suspicion. "The United States Department of Justice?"

Bolan and Constante understood each other. The soldier had been sent under the umbrella of the United States Department of Justice as Agent Matthew Cooper, a DOJ "observer" of the current political crisis. However, if that were true he would be spending his time with diplomats, politicians and lawyers rather than standing ankle-deep in the silt of the Laguna San José with a lowly homicide inspector. The title and the job description were phony and both men knew it. All Constante knew was that the Man had come to his island, and apparently the inspector thought it was about time.

"Give me a name," Bolan said.

"What kind of name, *señor?*" The inspector asked innocently.

"Why, the name of the worst son of a bitch in San Juan."

"Oh!" Constante brightened. "That is easy. The name you want is Yotuel d'Nico."

"I think I'll go have a talk with this Yotuel."

Constante grinned happily. "I will light a candle for you."

2

"So who's this Yotuel, anyway?" Bolan asked.

The bar stools around Bolan emptied as if he were radioactive. The bartender was short, fat, potbellied, bald and missing his front teeth. He also had a cursive letter *N* for *La Neta* tattooed on the back of his hand between his right thumb and forefinger. He looked Bolan up and down and leaned in close. "Hey, gringo, why don't you finish your beer and fuck off?"

Bolan finished his beer and ignored the invitation. "I mean, is he some kind of tough son of a bitch or something?"

The bartender elaborately washed his hands in the sink and muttered, "You dig your own grave" under his breath in Spanish.

"All the way to China, baby," agreed Bolan. He pushed his empty mug forward for another.

Strangely enough the bartender began refilling Bolan's glass. He smiled without an ounce of warmth. "Did you say…baby?"

"You bet your ass," Bolan agreed.

"You should be careful of using that word in this place. Bebito Jesus might be listening."

Bolan took the bait and the refilled mug. "We all have a friend in little baby Jesus."

"No." The bartender kept on smiling. "Not you, my friend."

There was no mirror behind the bar. Bolan had been aware of people in the dark booths in the back, and he had heard someone walking up behind him. He was somewhat surprised to find himself suddenly in shadow as if there were a solar eclipse in the barroom. Bolan swiveled his bar stool and behind him was Bebito Jesus.

There was nothing little nor Christlike about the be-hemoth looming over him. The man had to have topped six-foot ten, and his frame was sheathed in sumo-wrestler-sized rolls of fat. He looked like a cartoon character, but there was nothing funny about the look in his eye or the bass rumble of his voice. "Fuck you."

Bolan blew the froth off the top of his mug, and it slopped onto the giant's sandaled feet. He raised his mug in toast. "And your mother."

Bebito blinked. It was perhaps the first time anyone had said that to him in his life. Bolan didn't underestimate his opponent, but the Puerto Rican, on the other hand, seemed to be fatally underestimating Bolan. He slowly reached out with one spatulate hand and gathered up the front of the big American's shirt in his fist and began lifting him out of his seat. Bolan rose and snapped the stacked leather heel of his dress shoe down into his adversary's left big toe. Bebito's shoulders cringed and his eyes went blank with the sudden shock. Bolan took the opportunity to stomp down again and break his other big toe. Bebito gasped and stooped toward his pain. This brought his face on par with Bolan's. The Exe-cutioner snapped his forehead forward and shattered Bebito's cheekbone. The man's eyes rolled back in his head.

The behemoth toppled backward. Bolan sat back down at the bar. He hadn't spilled a drop of beer. "So, what were we talking about? Oh, yeah, well, you know? They call this Yotuel guy the Lion but he sounds like a real pussy to me."

"Mister..." The bartender stared at Bolan in almost total incomprehension. "You'd better leave."

"Yeah." Bolan put down his beer mug and dropped a twenty on the bar. "Tell this Lion freak I'll be back tomorrow, same time."

Bolan walked out into the street. Constante still leaned against the front fender of his black, unmarked Crown Victoria police car. This was one of the most dangerous neighborhoods in San Juan and the lanky inspector ate a Cuban sandwich and drank a Budweiser tall boy from a six-pack sitting on the hood like he owned the place. "Did you speak to Yotuel?"

"No, but I stepped on a few of the right toes," Bolan answered.

"I heard a crash. I almost came in."

"I ran into Bebito."

Constante started in surprise. He clearly knew the giant. "Bebito Jesus? What happened?"

Bolan shrugged. "That was the crash."

The inspector was impressed. "He assaulted you?"

"It didn't get that far."

The inspector looked sidelong at Bolan. "Is he dead?"

"No, but he needs to go see his podiatrist."

"Ah, well, it begins." Constante sighed happily.

BOLAN AND THE INSPECTOR drove through the night. The violent street protests of the day had given way to candlelit vigils in the plazas. Puerto Rican rock bands and rappers played freedom benefits. Professors and students made dramatic oratory. The guitar playing, speech making and talk over megaphones of a greater Puerto Rico were counterpointed by the darkened and looted storefronts and the smoldering and burning cars on the streets. The inspector had driven to a number of bars and spoken to informants. Bolan had not been privy to the conversations nor had he inquired. Right now it was Constante's play.

"Well, amigo, I will tell you." The inspector turned to him now. "It appears that Yotuel is very angry with you."

"So I would imagine," Bolan admitted.

"He is also aware that I was standing outside the bar while you impugned his reputation and destroyed his enforcer in insulting fashion." The inspector paused and then said, "I gather you are armed?"

Bolan had full war loads at the DOJ building, three safehouses and every military base on the island. He tapped the Smith & Wesson Centennial revolver in a cross-draw holster beneath his shirt. A lightweight titanium model of the same gun rode in an ankle holster. He simply said, "I have a gun."

"Well, I think it is going to be a bad night in old San Juan, amigo. Would you like to get a bigger gun? I think I would like a bigger gun myself."

"I'm your humble servant in all things," Bolan said.

Constante spit the stub of his cigarette out the window and punched the cigarette lighter on the console. "I suspect the opposite it true." He took the car back toward the capital police building and pulled into the underground parking lot. Men in uniform and plain clothes nodded at Constante as they went through a series of basement catacombs and finally came to a room with a counter guarded by thick bulletproof glass. The man behind the glass looked like an accountant except that the forearms revealed by his rolled-up sleeves were built like bowling pins and his fingernails were blackened by accumulated gun grease that would take industrial solvents to clean away.

"Mono!" The inspector grinned at the armorer. "I need guns!"

Mono turned a measuring eye on Bolan and then sighed in amusement at Constante. "Flaco Ordones was here. He already checked out the BAR. He said it was on your authorization." *Flaco* was Spanish slang for *skinny*. BAR was the U.S. military acronym for Browning Automatic Rifle. It seemed the inspector was serious about getting bigger guns.

Mono shook his head. "You know, Inspector, strictly speaking, only the SWAT team can check out weapons without clearance from above."

The inspector lit another cigarette and one for Mono as well. He sighed and blew smoke into the ceiling light. "You know something, Cooper? There was a time when a Puerto Rican cop could get anything he needed just by asking. Of course, there was always very little to be had…but you could get it."

Bolan nodded sympathetically. Inspector Constante was an old-school Puerto Rican cop. He came from a lineage that kicked doors, cracked heads and squeezed suspects. As Puerto Rico modernized, his day was swiftly coming to a close.

Constante warmed to his subject. "Now it is all forms, subcommittees, review boards, and, Heavenly Father help us, after-action reports." He turned on the armorer. "Are you going to make me fill out forms in triplicate, Mono? Do I need to form a subcommittee to recommend my course of action?"

Mono regarded Constante drily. "Might I inquire as to what your course of action may be?"

"Oh, is that all?" Constante nodded toward Bolan. "Me and the gringo are going to clean up Puerto Rico. He already started with the Taino bar. Apparently he used Bebito as a mop."

Mono blinked at Bolan several times. "You will need guns." The armorer turned back to his racks and workbenches and came back with a pair of ancient and cracked leather violin cases. Inspector Constante opened one of the cases and stared lovingly at the contents. "You know, my friend, Puerto Rico has always been the United States' poor little cousin. I, myself, as a young man, was in the Puerto Rican National Guard. We did not receive M-16 rifles and M-60 machine guns. We received WWII Garand rifles, Browning Automatic Rifles, military surplus. I was Military Police, and my unit received Thompson submachine guns."

Constante racked the action. The wooden stock was dinged and stained and much of the weapon's gunmetal blue finish was missing, but the action racked as slick as oil on glass and bespoke Mono's faithful maintenance. Constante ran a fond hand over the ancient weapon. "You know it?"

Bolan had found a Tommy gun in his hand a surprising number of times. "I'm familiar with it."

"I believe you are." He nodded at the other case and Bolan examined the weapon. "How many spare magazines would you like?"

Bolan loaded the weapon, racked it and flicked on the safety. "How about eighteen?"

"In the army we were generally issued nine."

"How many street soldiers can d'Nico call on?" Bolan countered.

"Hundreds. Do you intend to take on all of *La Neta* by yourself?"

"No, just select elements of it, and with your help," Bolan said.

Constante turned to the armorer. "Mono, thirty-six magazines, if you don't mind, and enough ammunition to load all of them, as well as some spare boxes."

Mono raised his eyebrows slightly at the request and re-treated back into his catacombs. Constante put his weapon back in its case. "Where are you staying?"

"I'm renting a house in *La Perla*."

The inspector made a face. *La Perla* was one of the worst slums in San Juan and ruthlessly ruled by gang culture. "You taunt the Lion, then you climb into his jaws."

"Well, you know how they say you should keep your enemies close."

"They do not say you should move in next to them," Constante scowled.

"I don't think I'll be staying long."

Mono brought them their ammo and they walked out without filling any forms. As they walked back to the parking garage, Constante began speaking quietly. "You know? It is hard to be a policeman in Puerto Rico."

Bolan nodded. It was a little known fact that perhaps other than Mexico City or Moscow there was no more dangerous place to be a police officer.

Most Americans had no idea of how bad it was. If Americans thought of their commonwealth neighbor in the Caribbean, they thought of blue water, golden sand and partying. It was a common vacation destination for East Coasters and an alternative honeymoon spot.

For the people who lived there violence was endemic. Since the rise of the cocaine trade in the 1980s the island had become a major transshipment point for Colombian cocaine and increasingly a heroin funnel. The Puerto Rican gang and crime cultures had risen with them. People on the island made roughly a third of the average income of the poorest mainland states, and it was reflected in their police force. They were ill-equipped and understaffed, and corruption in the force was as endemic as the violence in the streets.

"You intend to go against the crime gangs and the revolutionaries?" the inspector asked.

"I do."

"I am ashamed to admit it, but there are those within the force who support what is happening, not out of patriotic sentiment, but because they know if we become an independent nation the potential for profit in bribery will skyrocket. The drug dealers and the gangs know this as well and are already lining pockets," the inspector said.

Bolan suspected nothing less.

"You will need a force of cops who cannot be corrupted or bought. Those who will not be afraid to bend rules, if not break them outright," Constante concluded.

"It'd be helpful," Bolan said.

Constante gestured at his car and the woman leaning against it. "Then behold your second recruit."

The woman turned. She was short, redheaded, darkly tanned with broad shoulders and an eye-popping bust line that was barely restrained by a blue T-shirt. A corset-thin waist cut what would have been a blocky figure into an hourglass.

"May I present Detective Guistina Gustolallo. She works Vice."

Bolan could have guessed that. He also noted the Mossberg 12-gauge semi-automatic shotgun crooked in one elbow like she was about to go duck hunting. Her dark eyes looked Bolan up and down in open suspicion. "Yo, Vincente." The detective popped her gum. "Who's the gringo?"

"Why, he is the man who put Bebito in the hospital and called Yotuel d'Nico a *puto*."

Bolan held out his hand. "Nice to meet you, Detective."

"Detective…" The woman ignored Bolan's hand and rose up on her toes to kiss Bolan on both cheeks Latin style. "People I like call me Gustolallo. And you, Blue Eyes, qualify."

Constante lit another cigarette. "Where is Roldan?"

The woman shrugged. "Roldan is off duty in an hour. Ordones said to call him when you need him."

"Tell them to meet us in *La Perla*." Constante turned to Bolan. "Give her the address."

Bolan gave it to her, and Detective Gustolallo began speaking rapid-fire Spanish into her cell phone. They piled into Constante's car and headed down toward the water. *La Perla* was anything but "The Pearl" of metropolitan San Juan. Beneath the four-hundred-year-old walls and turrets of the fortifications built by the Spanish explorer Ponce de Leon, shacks and hovels leaned against one another. Even at this late hour stick-thin children wandered around in rags and picked at piles of garbage right next to feral dogs. Other piles of garbage burned or were being burned in the hovels for fuel. *La Perla* was just about the worst barrio in San Juan.

Inspector Constante's shiny black Crown Victoria was clearly an anomaly. Bolan noticed cell phones in the hands of some of the children marking them as runners for the local drug dealers. They watched the black Ford with wary eyes and punched presets as they drifted back into the shadows. A trio of transvestite prostitutes made catcalls and a few improbable offers at the car and then grabbed their phones once it passed. *La Perla*'s grapevine was lighting up.

"We're about to get hit," Bolan opined.

"Oh, undoubtedly," the inspector agreed. "I gather you made no attempt at subtlety when you moved in to the neighborhood.

"None whatsoever," Bolan admitted.

Gustolallo popped her gum in the back seat and the safety on her shotgun clicked off.

Bolan saw a pair of headlights suddenly light up an alley ahead. "Here it comes."

Gustolallo sang out from the back seat. "We got one behind!"

Bolan flicked the safety off his Thompson. "They're gonna go for the pin."

The pin was another gift from the drug gangs of Mexico, mostly used for assassinating police officers. Drive-bys were uncertain at best, but a couple of SUVs could surround and stop a car on a narrow street or in a parking lot, and then the men with automatic rifles would spill out of all doors and fill the pinned vehicle full of lead. A gleaming silver Lincoln Navigator shot into the street ahead of them with tires squealing. A tangerine-and-black Honda Element fishtailed into position behind them. On *La Perla*'s narrow, twisting lanes there was no room to maneuver. Constante pushed buttons on his console and the Crown Vic's windows rolled down and the custom sunroof rolled back. Constante spit out his cigarette and grinned defiantly at the silver SUV blocking their escape. "I'm gonna ram him."

"No," Bolan commanded.

"No?"

"Hit Reverse. Hit the guy behind us. He's lighter and only has four cylinders."

"Ah!" The tires screamed on the cobblestones as the inspector stood on the breaks and threw the vehicle into Reverse. "Hold on!"

The Ford shot backward into the Element. The glare of the headlights filling the Crown Vic's interior smashed out as the Honda crumpled like the cardboard box it was shaped like. The Crown Vic's V-8 engine roared as it drove the stricken little SUV back. Bolan rose up through the sunroof. Glass erupted in geysers from the Honda's windshield as Bolan painted a 15-round pattern over the driver's position and a second one over the glass covering the man riding shotgun. Gustolallo's shotgun hammered rapidly five times on semiauto, and the windshield failed utterly and sagged backward into the SUV's interior.

Nothing inside the Element was moving.

Bolan slapped in a fresh magazine. "Forward! Go! Go! Go!" He dropped back down and put on his seat belt as Constante slammed the vehicle into Drive and put the pedal to the metal. The huge SUV before them had pulled out at an angle to block the lane. Now the driver was desperately trying to execute a three-point turn to face the oncoming Ford while the passengers waved their arms and screamed.

The Crown Vic hit the Navigator broadside at fifty miles per hour. The impact was brutal, but Bolan had braced himself and the air bag deployed against him. He got out of his seat belt, and clicked open his switchblade and slashed away the deflating air bag. The windshield had gone opaque with cracks, and Bolan's door refused to budge. He rose up through the sunroof. The Navigator was wrapped around the front bumper of the vehicle. The driver and back passenger doors were folded in and not moving. Bolan bent back as one of the men in the back seat of the Navigator tried to fire at him with an M-16. The window erupted outward, but the space was too cramped inside the SUV for the gunman to fire effectively.

Bolan had no such restraints.

The Thompson ripped into life. Constante leaped out from behind the wheel as his weapon joined the crescendo. The doors facing away flew open and men piled out of the Navigator. Bolan jumped onto the hood, then leaped to the roof of the SUV. Two men turned and raised their rifles, but Bolan burned them down with a burst through their chests before they could fire. A young man with a clearly broken arm fell to his knees and raised his working hand piteously. *"Madre de Dios! Por favor! Por favor!"*

Bolan kept the smoking muzzle of his weapon pointed between the young man's eyes. Gustolallo came around the SUV and kicked the surrendering punk onto his stomach. He screamed in pain as she twisted both arms back and cuffed him. Constante looked into one of the Navigator's shattered windows and made a face at the carnage within. "Clear."

Bolan stood atop the SUV and surveyed the area. Dogs were barking. Women and children in the hovels and tenements were screaming. Sirens began wailing in the distance. The transvestites clapped their hands and whistled. It had been a fine show, and they clearly liked the big gringo with the big gun standing on top of the Navigator's shattered shell.

Gustolallo yanked the young man up to his knees and the inspector smiled delightedly. Bolan eyed the cringing punk. "You know him?"

"Indeed!" Constante leaned in and leered in the young man's face. "This is Nacho d'Nico!"

Bolan smiled coldly. "Yotuel's little brother?"

"His *punkito* little brother," the inspector emphasized. "What's the matter, Nacho? You don't look so good."

Between shock, pain and naked terror, Nacho looked just about ready to soil himself. Bolan jumped to the hood, then down to the street. The sirens were getting closer. "I don't think your car is going any place."

"No," the inspector agreed. "And neither shall I. I will stay here. I will say I was alone and was attacked, then killed my attackers. You and Gustolallo take the punk to your place. If we bring him in, he will only be out on bail tomorrow. I will join you shortly."

It was as good a plan as any. Bolan nodded and Nacho shrieked as Gustolallo yanked him to his feet. Constante lit a cigarette and leaned against his totaled vehicle to wait, apparently oblivious of the gas pooling everywhere.

Bolan and the detective took Nacho d'Nico for a little walk through the neighborhood. It was going to be a long night.

3

Nacho whimpered, then muttered in rapid Puerto Rican slang. His face was pale and he was sweating bullets. Bolan checked his watch. He'd sweated him for about an hour and he could guess what he was saying. Gustolallo sat across from Nacho at the ratty little kitchen table of Bolan's flat and stared at him like he was a bug. Bolan had uncuffed him and put his arm in a sling, but Nacho was still very unhappy. He had stopped with the threats about half an hour ago and Bolan expected him to move into the begging phase right on schedule. The big American checked his watch again.

Gustolallo frowned. "I won't lie to you, Blue. The inspector could be in a lot of trouble."

Nacho snarled with renewed courage. "The inspector is fucking dead!"

Nacho shrieked as Gustolallo lunged across the table and punched him in the sling. It seemed the women cops in Puerto Rico played as rough as the men. Bolan held up a restraining hand and the detective uncocked her fist and sat back down. Nacho whimpered and cradled his arm. Bolan figured the diminutive young gangster was just about ready. Bolan had stopped at a corner kiosk on the way to the flat and picked up a few interrogation aids. He looked at Nacho and sighed sympathetically. "That hurt?"

"Yeah, it fucking hurts!" Nacho instantly flinched beneath Gustolallo's glare.

Bolan reached into the kitchen cabinet and pulled out a bottle. He poured a drinking glass half full of clear liquid and slid it within Nacho's reach. "For the pain. Sorry I don't have anything stronger."

The younger d'Nico lunged for the 151 proof Don Q rum and gulped it like water. Bolan took out a pack of Marlboros from his pocket. "Cigarette?"

Nacho's gratitude was almost pathetic as Bolan lit him one and put it between his lips. Bolan refilled his glass. Gustolallo shot him a frosty look and he poured her a shot, as well. Bolan took a fatherly tone. "Nacho, you're in a lot of trouble."

"I want a lawyer."

Bolan shrugged. "Why?"

"This is illegal! You can't hold me!"

Bolan cocked his head at the punk. "I'll make things very clear to you. I'm not a cop. I can do anything I want."

Nacho blanched. He looked desperately at Gustolallo. "She's a cop!"

The detective popped her gum. "I'm off duty. I'm riding you for the fun of it."

Nacho hissed. *"Puta de—"* He howled as Gustolallo's fist pounded his arm just above his broken elbow. A second jab followed it to his nose.

Bolan poured Nacho another drink. The young man couldn't have weighed more than a 120 pounds naked and dripping wet. Between shock and an empty stomach, Bolan expected to have a well-lubricated *La Neta* gangster very shortly.

A voice called out from the street outside in Spanish. *"Hello the house!"*

Gustolallo nodded. "Ordones and Roldan."

Bolan still picked up his Thompson and held it low

along his side as he unlocked the kitchen door. "Come ahead! Through the kitchen!"

Two men walked into the kitchen. One was as tall as Bebito Jesus and had to stoop to come through the door, but unlike the giant *La Neta* enforcer, this man was gaunt to the point of emaciation. His tropical white suit hung upon his giant bones like a scarecrow. He had the sad, brown eyes and pale, tired complexion of a man who slept away most days without seeing the sun. He carried something long and bulky wrapped in a brightly patterned native blanket across his broad shoulders. The man behind him was dark-skinned and built like a middle-weight. He radiated aggressive energy to the point that Bolan wondered if the short-cropped, tight, metallic-brown coils of hair coming out of his head might be nerve endings. He was carrying a rifle case and instantly shot a suspicious look at Gustolallo and Bolan. The two men took turns kissing Gustolallo in greeting. The giant held out his hand to Bolan. The soldier's hand disappeared in the tall man's grip but it was warm and friendly. His voice was a Spanish baritone. "Sergeant Ernesto Ordones, but you may call me Ordones."

"Cooper." Bolan said. The younger man in turn gave Bolan the bone crusher, and the two of them pumped vise grips for a moment. The giant sighed. "May I introduce Officer Ruzzo Roldan."

Roldan released Bolan's hand but continued to glare at him. His accent was thick enough to cut with a knife. "I heard of you."

Bolan shrugged. "What did you hear?"

"Word on the street is you busted up a bar. Word is you busted up Bebito Jesus and called out Yotuel d'Nico. Word is you shot up a bunch of d'Nico's men in *La Perla*. Word is Inspector Constante is getting grilled at headquarters right now because of your Yanqui cowboy bullshit." Roldan shook his head as he took in Nacho. "Word on the street is you're holding the Lion's little brother. Word is everyone knows this address, and the word is the Lion is pissed. Word is you're in a lot of trouble."

Bolan turned to Ordones. "Word is you got a BAR."

The tall man's skull nearly hit the ceiling as he threw back his head and laughed and tapped his bundle "*Sí*, amigo. I just happen to have one."

Roldan wasn't amused. "So what's your plan? Sit here in this shithole and wait for d'Nico to hit this place with an army?"

Bolan nodded. "That's about it."

Ordones turned to Gustolallo. "You know? I like this gringo."

Gustolallo's smile was predatory. "Me, too."

Roldan's anger cooled to something cold and unpleasant. "I'll tell you something that maybe you won't think is so funny."

"What's that?" Bolan asked.

"Word is moving through the department. *Los Macheteros* say anyone who helps the gringo, and I'm pretty sure that means you, is a traitor."

Nacho roared drunkenly. "That's right! Fucking traitors! Dead fucking traitors!"

Roldan ignored the outburst. "A traitor to Puerto Rico and a traitor to all Boricuas, and I'll tell you something for nothing, Cooper, a lot of the cops are taking that real seriously. You're an outsider. The inspector has already been dragged in and lost friends over this. No one wants you here."

"The inspector is fully on board, and he was laughing when I left him," Bolan countered. "And you came to *La*

Perla, off duty." He nodded at the rifle case. "And you brought your gun."

"I came to support the inspector. I was a gangbanger back in the day, but I was no *La Neta puto.*" He shot a scathing look at Nacho and the punk flinched. The officer pounded his chest twice with his fist in the sign of solidarity. "I was Latin Kings and headed straight to jail or the grave. Inspector Constante got me out of that shit. Got me to finish high school. He risked his reputation to sponsor me when I applied to join the force. I came to support him." Roldan thrust out his jaw. "Not your pretty pink Yanqui ass."

"Did the inspector tell you to do what I tell you until he gets back from headquarters?" Bolan inquired.

The pained look that crossed Roldan's face was confirmation.

"Roldan, I'm here to wipe out *La Neta, Los Macheteros* and anybody else who wants to decide the fate of Puerto Rico with a gun rather than a vote. You in or out?"

"I'm—" Roldan spent several moments controlling his temper "—in."

"If you boys are done, we got stuff to do," Gustolallo stated.

Just then Bolan took out his phone as it vibrated in his pocket. Kurtzman's text message scrolled across the screen.

striker, you have company

The phone's screen took up just about all of its length. Bolan's thumb moved across the touch screen, and a real-time satellite image of his house and the surrounding neighborhood appeared. Half a dozen vehicles denoted by red outlines were surrounding the building. Armed men were deploying out of them. The image wasn't perfect but he saw nothing bigger than automatic weapons. "We have company. Platoon strength. Coming in on all sides."

Roldan pulled an M-16 from his rifle bag and Ordones unwrapped his BAR and deployed the bipod. Bolan pulled a tab off the left wrist of his jacket to expose a Velcro panel. He slapped his phone onto it and took up his Thompson.

A voice out on the street called out in Spanish. *"Give us Nacho!"*

"He isn't worth it!" Bolan called back. "I promise you!"

Nacho looked like he was about to say something, but Gustolallo pantomimed ramming the steel strut of her folding-stock shotgun into his elbow and he thought better of it.

"And the Yanqui!" the voice shouted. More followed but the Puerto Rican slang was too fast and too furious for Bolan to get more than the gist of it, but that was enough. They wanted Nacho and they wanted him now. Everyone else in the house was a traitor to Puerto Rico. Unless they stood down, both they and their families would die. The voice switched to English. "Hey, Yanqui! Go home! You can live! Don't make me come in there!"

Ordones laid the BAR across the table and aimed it at the front door. Bolan cupped his hands and called out, "Door's open!"

Dozens of automatic weapons opened up out on the street. Plaster fell from the ceiling, and the ancient brick walls chipped and cracked beneath the barrage of lead. Bolan noted that the weapons sounded as though they were 9 mms, and they all had the same firing signature. He pushed Nacho to the floor and then glanced at the screen of his phone. "Ordones! I got about six men behind a car directly across the street from the front door!"

Ordones nodded and the thudding of the big .30-caliber machine gun eclipsed the sound of the submachine guns out on the street. The 30-06 rifle bullets sailed through the front door, the car across the street and the men taking cover behind it. Bolan saw four men fall on his screen and two more run headlong for the beach.

Kurtzman text messaged him.

heat signatures behind you

Bolan looked at his wrist and saw the bright flickering on the infrared filter. Five men were running crouched alongside a car, making their approach down the alley behind the house. Each man held something that was burning—Molotov cocktails. Four more gunners trotted behind, blasting away with weapons as they came. "Ordones! I got a vehicle coming directly behind us! Roldan! Gustolallo! Watch the front!"

Ordones turned and rammed the muzzle of his BAR through the kitchen window glass and started firing. Bolan kicked open the kitchen door and brought his Thompson to his shoulder. Bullets hailed against the back of the house, but the soldier kept his sights on the firebombers. A bullet slammed into Bolan's side but his soft body armor held. His return burst took off the top of the gunman's head. Rum bottles filled with gasoline and detergent sailed through the air.

Bolan raised his sights and began touching off bursts from the Thompson and broke apart bottles in the air like a skeet shooter busting clays. Sheets of fire fell across the alley and across the hood of the Cadillac as it rolled on. Bolan took out three of the four projectiles, and his weapon clacked open on empty as the fourth sailed on in a near-perfect football spiral.

Ordones snarled and yanked himself aside as the flaming bomb flew through the kitchen window a foot from his head. Nacho screamed as the Molotov cocktail sailed across the room and broke apart at his feet. Bolan slammed a fresh magazine into his weapon and kept firing. "Gustolallo!"

Gustolallo yanked up the ratty kitchen rug and jumped on top of Nacho. She swore a blue streak as Nacho howled and flailed while she tried to smother the fire. The BAR continued, tearing through the Cadillac as if it didn't exist, and Bolan shot any gangster who exposed himself. Bolan slammed in a fresh magazine as the Caddy's front fender scraped against the alley wall and it rolled to a halt. The gunfire in the back of the house came to an abrupt end. Puddles of fire were everywhere. Flame licked up the walls of the alley, and the Cadillac burned like a fallen tombstone. The alley resembled a side entrance to hell.

Bolan heard the thump and hiss of ignition. The Cadillac was riddled with high-power rifle holes, and the jellied fuel of the firebombs was crawling all through it. Bolan slammed the kitchen door shut. "Down!"

The Cadillac's fuel tank detonated like a bomb. The door rattled on its hinges, and heat blasted through the shattered kitchen window hot enough to singe skin. Nacho screamed, his right foot kicked out from under the rug and clocked Gustolallo in the face. She rolled backward, stunned as Nacho got to his feet and ran screaming out of the kitchen with bits of fire still flickering on his feet.

Gustolallo kneeled and snarled past her bloody lips and nose. *"Bastardo!"*

Bolan shoved down the barrel of her shotgun.

Roldan's M-16 fired on rapid semiauto from the front of the house. "More firebombs out front! We got—" He stared back in surprise as Nacho ran screaming past him. Bolan made a quick throat-cutting motion. Roldan caught it and let Nacho get past. When the Executioner motioned with his own weapon to shoot high, Roldan's M-16 snarled on full-auto and he roared, "Get back here, you son of a bitch!"

Nacho sailed straight through the front window and

onto the porch. Bolan advanced, firing. One of the three firebombers out front fell with one of Roldan's bullets in his chest. The other two threw their bottles, but Roldan cracked one in flight and the other fell short and broke apart on the cobblestones in front of the house. Bolan checked his screen. Three of the four surviving vehicles were pulling out and driving away. Men on foot were fleeing in all directions. Nacho was heading due north and didn't look like he was going to stop until he hit Bermuda.

The back of the house was beginning to burn in earnest.

Ordones rose, reloaded and handed his handkerchief to Gustolallo. She ruefully held it up to her bloody nose and stared over it at Bolan. "You're just gonna let the little son of a bitch go?"

Roldan glared over his shoulder from his position covering the front. "Yeah! What the fuck was that all about?"

Ordones, on the other hand, glanced at Bolan slyly. "You're tracking our little friend, aren't you?"

"Yeah." Bolan shrugged. "I put a bug in his sling while I was binding him up. I figured I'd like to see where he runs to."

"He will run to his big brother, *El León,*" Ordones suggested.

"I'm hoping."

Roldan grinned uncharacteristically. *"Fantástico."*

Bolan turned to more immediate matters. "We've got to get out of here. As officers in the Puerto Rican police force, I'm afraid your superiors are going to want you to report in for questioning, and it's only going to get worse the longer you stick around me."

Ordones folded the bipod of his weapon and rewrapped it in its blanket. "As of now I consider myself AWOL."

Gustolallo's bloody nose wrinkled. "What's AWOL?"

"Absent Without Leave," Ordones replied.

Gustolallo nodded decisively. "Me, too."

Everyone looked at Roldan. The young cop was still grinning. "I been waiting for this all my life. Let's do it!"

Bolan nodded. He had a crew, and they had been bloodied in battle.

Now it was time to take the war to the enemy.

4

Bolan cruised the BMW F650 Dakar motorcycle through the highlands. The capital city of San Juan was a pocket of stars below. He checked the screen of the phone attached to his wrist as they passed gated roads that led to the mansions of Puerto Rico's rich and powerful. Yotuel d'Nico had reached the top echelons of the *La Neta* gangs, and not surprisingly, *El León* kept a home near the top of the mountain so he could look down upon his hunting grounds. Detective Gustolallo leaned in to Bolan's back as he brought the bike to a stop. "Thank you for bringing me."

"Well, I might need some backup," he said as he got off the bike. "Besides, Ordones won't fit on the back of my bike and I figure Roldan wouldn't feel much like spooning with me."

"After what happened in *La Perla* I think Roldan would be your date to the prom if you asked him."

"He's a real hard charger," Bolan said.

"Oh, he's always asking for the most dangerous assignments."

Bolan took in the cool wind of the Puerto Rican highlands. He could see d'Nico's house in the distance. At least now he knew where his enemy slept.

Leaning against the bike, Bolan frowned as he remembered his conversation with their quarry in *La Perla*.

"Nacho threw out a name I didn't recognize, Orishas Chango. Mean anything to you?"

"*Orishas? Chango?* That's Santería shit. It came from Africa when the Spanish brought in slaves. *Orishas* are like spirits or gods. It's like Haitian voodoo but different. When *La Neta* and the other gangs aren't busy claiming their Taino Indian ancestry they're flirting with Santería. They like to claim the *orishas* give them power, but most of them are posers rather than true believers. They mostly just like to wear the jewelry, sport the tattoos and sprinkle chicken blood around to scare people."

Bolan flexed his Spanish. "So *Orishas de Chango* would be spirits of the spirit?"

Gustolallo poked him in the side. "It only sounds redundant because you're a Yanqui. What it means to someone on the streets of San Juan is that they're spirits of the spirit Chango, like his outriders or emissaries or something."

"So what's this Chango dude all about?"

"Oh, he's got a lot of qualities, or aspects. Chango's the SkyFather, god of thunder and lightning, god of music and dance, of justice, war and a dozen other things. But since the name was coming out of Nacho's drunken piehole, I'm thinking he was talking about Chango's aspect as the god of revenge. His symbol is a double-headed ax."

Bolan turned to the detective. "Chango is the god of justice and revenge?"

"Yeah—"

"And his symbol is a double-headed African war ax?"

"Yeah, and?" Gustolallo asked.

"And people have been turning up without heads in the San Jose lagoon for the last month."

"Jesus…"

"I think this is bigger than just the street gangs and the

Macheteros. I think there's a new group of enforcers in town and they're our *Orishas de Chango.*"

"Jesus. If the gangs aren't running these guys then who is?"

"The drug cartels, or maybe the independence terrorists, or both. I don't know yet, but I've been getting an outside-orchestration vibe in what's been happening. Someone wants to rip Puerto Rico right off its moorings, and they're playing all the local political and race cards"

"Okay, now you're scaring the shit out of me."

Bolan excused himself and stepped away from Gustolallo as he tapped icons on the phone attached to his sleeve. The Farm's mission controller, Barbara Price, appeared on a screen inset the size of a ravioli. Her brows rose sleepily as she peered into the webcam. "What's going on, Striker?"

"Barb, everyone's been assuming that the recent beheadings in Puerto Rico are just copycat killings taken from the Mexican cartels. My problem is local CSI has done all the autopsies. I don't think they're totally reliable. Some may even be in on a fix. I need you to arrange a clean forensics team to reexamine any of the headless bodies still available."

Price was used to strange, late-night requests from the field but even she had to admit she was intrigued. "To determine…?"

"To determine whether the decapitations were performed with a machete or an ax." Bolan had seen enough headless bodies to know there would be a difference. "A machete would make a chopping wound and probably take several cuts. An ax would leave impact and shearing trauma in the surrounding tissues, and used with any skill would be a one-cut proposition."

"I'll have Hal contact San Juan's special agent in charge."

"The FBI is mostly local. I'd rather have you get in touch with the CIA station chief."

Price sighed. Despite all efforts to the contrary since the events of 9/11, inter-service rivalry was still rife in the U.S. intelligence and law-enforcement communities. Many Puerto Ricans considered themselves Americans, and both the Puerto Rican law enforcement and the public at large believed, and not without some merit, that the CIA presence on the island was there to spy on the citizenry. "That could ruffle some feathers."

Bolan shrugged. "I don't care."

"Hal's going to care." Price sighed. "So will the State Department, and probably the President."

"They'll care more about who's behind all this."

She knew Bolan was right. "I'll have an autopsy report for you within twenty-four hours."

"Thanks, Barb. Striker out."

THE LION LOOKED at his kid brother, and what he saw didn't please him. Nacho had turned eighteen that year and for six months had been pestering incessantly for an opportunity to move up. Yotuel had finally relented. Killing Inspector Constante, which had needed doing for some time anyway, was to have been Nacho's ticket into the big leagues. It had turned into a slaughter. *El León* sighed heavily. So had the rescue operation to get Nacho back. The young man sat flinching and unable to look into his big brother's eyes. The room was dark except for two small ceiling lamps that illuminated each man at the table. Other men hovered back in the darkness. Yotuel eyed his brother again. Nacho's nose was broken, his arm was in a sling and his shoes and his pants were scorched black. Yotuel's nose wrinkled and his down-curved lips curled with contempt.

Nacho stank of rum.

Yotuelo sighed again. "Brother, what am I to do with you?"

The two men could not have been more different. Nacho was a sack of chicken bones in a very expensive designer track suit. Yotuel, *El León,* looked every inch his nickname. He was a lion of a man, over six feet tall with a wide brow and a protruding lower jaw. He'd had his hair straightened, and it fell around his shoulders in a blue-black mane in the style of the Taino Indian ancestry he claimed. Taino tribal tattooing crawled down his heavily muscled arms entwined with *La Neta* prison tattoos. His symbol of power was a seventeenth-century Spanish lance head he carried thrust under his belt. The socket was wrapped with leather cord to make a hilt. Catholic saints' medals and beaded Santería fetishes hung from it in braids. The two-foot steel blade was pitted and brown with age execpt for the edges, which gleamed like mercury from sharpening.

He drew the antique iron and began cleaning his finger-nails with the needle-sharp point. "Tell me about the cops."

Nacho eyed the spear blade nervously. "One was an old man, but tall, tall like a tree, like he should've played in the NBA or something."

"Flaco Ordones." Yotuelo nodded. He knew him. Ordones came on like a kindly grandfather with suspects, but he was the same old-school-style cop as Constante. "And the others?"

"I knew one of them." Anger kindled in Nacho's eyes. "That goddamn Roldan."

Yotuel knew Roldan by reputation. Ruzzo "el Santo" Roldan was a cop, reportedly unbribable and a former Latin King. As far as Yotuel was concerned, that was strike one, strike two and strike three.

"The other was that bitch, Gustolallo."

The Lion smiled slightly. Detective Guistina Gusto-lallo. The redheaded cop had used her beauty to run several very successful undercover stings against the Puerto Rican drug cartels until her face had become too well-known, and she had gone on to make detective. Like a lot of criminals in Puerto Rico, *El León* harbored some fantasies of getting his hands on Gustolallo when she wasn't wearing her badge and gun. Yotuel put those fantasies aside for later. "And the Yanqui?"

Nacho shuddered. "Mother of God, brother, you should have seen this dude."

"Brother, you were supposed to kill this dude," Yotuel stated.

Nacho stared glumly at his blackened sneakers.

"Perhaps you would like a second chance?"

What Nacho would've really liked was the first flight to Miami, where he could spend a couple of weeks getting lap dances, betting on jai alai and restoring his shattered nerves.

A long sigh rumbled out of Yotuel's thick chest. "But then, with what has happened tonight, perhaps it is best if we lie low for a little while."

Nacho nodded vigorously. He obviously thought lying low was an excellent plan.

"Tell you what, brother," Yotuel continued. "We need to get you out of sight for a while. I'm going to send you to Miami. We'll have a doctor fix your nose. Set your arm. Then you rest up. I'll send for you in a week and then we will kill this Yanqui asshole together."

Nacho sagged with relief. "Thank you, brother—I mean, yes! We will kill him! We will kill him together!"

"Yes." Yotuel nodded with more conviction than he felt. He turned to one of his men. "Raciel, go with him. Have

Mario fly you, and take Cuco. You two? You will have my little brother's back."

"Yes, Yotuel. Like he is our own little brother." Raciel was short, violent, built like a fire hydrant and he considered Nacho worse than useless. However, Raciel liked Florida, blond strippers and jai alai, and Nacho spent money like water. There were worse jobs than a one-week mission babysitting him in Miami. Raciel jerked his head at Nacho and they left the room.

A man came out of the shadows from behind Yotuel. He was knife-thin with brush-cut gray hair, and he radiated command presence. "Your little brother is a liability."

"I have known that for eighteen years," the Lion rumbled. He glared at his visitor. "What are you suggesting?"

The thin man smiled, but his flat black eyes were as cold as a shark's. "I am suggesting we turn him into an asset."

One normally cruel corner of Yotuel's mouth turned up in amusement. "If you can do that, then you really are an *orisha*."

The visitor's smile reached his eyes. "Oh, but I am."

5

Safehouse, San Juan

"The decapitations were performed wth an ax." Aaron "the Bear" Kurtzman transmitted some very gruesome autopsy photos of the bodies Bolan had witnessed being pulled from the lagoon. Technical medical data scrolled down a sidebar, listing vertebral splintering, soft tissue compression and shearing and frontal bruising of the trachea. Bits of wood had been compressed into the front of the remaining neck tissue. What it meant was that someone had bent the necks of three U.S. Military Policemen over a stump and taken their heads like they'd been splitting kindling.

Kurtzman highlighted some of the text. "There was metal residue in some of the sheared bone. The ax was made out of iron."

That was interesting. "Not steel?"

"No, the CIA had one of their metallurgy specialists run it. The weapon was smelted through traditional African methods." Kurtzman warmed to his subject. "The African Iron Age preceded Europe's by four centuries or more, but once they'd established their smelting methods they didn't change much. Smelting in sub-Saharan Africa was always artisanal and guarded by secretive guilds. Just about every piece forged, from an ax to a hoe blade to a spear point or even a cook pot, had to be individually commissioned. A single iron piece could take several days to manufacture. It stayed this way right up until the modern era. During the colonial period, European metal goods of all kinds flooded Africa. It was easier to buy or trade for a cheap tin pot than have an iron one commissioned. By the 1950s traditional blacksmithing in Africa had just about disappeared."

Bolan considered that. "So the weapon in question is an antique."

"Weapons, plural." Kurtzman smiled. "Between the bodies taken from the lagoon on your arrival and those of some cops from the week before we got at least three murder weapons in play. All antique, all iron, all clearly smelted by African methods. All probably between seventy-five to a hundred years old."

Bolan saw where Kurtzman was going. "If the *Orishas de Chango* are passing out antique African war axes to the members like party favors, then somewhere in the Caribbean we have some museums missing some pieces."

"We've already started on museums in Puerto Rico that have West African collections as well as collections of Santería and voodoo artifacts. We're hacking their computers, discreetly looking for traditional axes and cross-referencing for reports of stolen artifacts."

"Bear, the axes might not be stolen. The curator or people who work there may have given the weapons away if they were approached correctly. They might even be part of the movement. Check Puerto Rican police files for antiquarians, museum workers or culturalists who are under any sort of political suspicion."

"I'll have Barb contact the local—"

"Have Akira hack their files," Bolan countered, referring to one of the Stony Man Farm's top hackers. "We have strong reason to believe elements of local law enforcement are involved in what's going on, and a request like this could tip our hand. The majority of the cops aren't active in the revolution, but most of them are taking the warning not to cooperate with outside investigations seriously. Even if they don't actively obstruct us or give us away, they'll sit on their hands and push paper for days. I want Akira inside their network and getting the information we need ASAP."

"Gotcha."

"Thanks. What have we got on Yotuel?"

"Nothing." Kurtzman frowned. "He's gone underground. In fact, most of *La Neta* has gone to ground. People are still protesting and rioting in the streets but the gangs have suddenly gone as quiet as church mice."

"They're waiting for something," Bolan stated. "How's our little friend Nacho?"

"He's still in Miami. As requested, Miami-Dade has a loose tail on him."

"What's he been up to?"

Kurtzman snorted. "He likes strippers and betting on jai alai. He has two goons with him. One Raciel de Regla and Cuco Juanmanuel. Raciel is street muscle and a real piece of work. He did a nickel for aggravated assault against two police officers. Cuco's record is so clean it's creepy. Rumor is he's an enforcer. A real bump-in-the-night kind of guy." Kurtzman was suddenly suspicious. "Why?"

"Things are quiet here. I think I'll go goose Nacho and see what happens." Bolan turned to Gustolallo, where she sat on the couch drinking rum and coffee. "You want to go goose Nacho and see what happens?"

The detective's eyes gleamed. "Miami? Yeah."

"Bear, it looks like I'm going to Miami with Detective

Gustolallo. Have Barb get me the first flight to the mainland and coordinate me with the local law that's tailing Nacho."

"I'm on it."

Wahoo Lou's Double D, VIP room, Miami

BOLAN WATCHED AS A woman bumped and ground her posterior inches from Detective Gustolallo's face as rap music pumped at eardrum-shattering decibels.

Gustolallo caught Bolan looking. She pointed a finger at him over her rum and Coke and shouted over the noise. "You know? I don't swing this way, but I can see why you guys dig this!"

Bolan sipped his fifteen-year-old single-malt whiskey and shrugged as six feet of Icelandic inbreeding gyrated to gain his attention. "Yeah."

The VIP room was a long balcony encased in one-way mirror glass. Bolan watched Nacho and his muscle downstairs. Nacho had a bandage over his nose and was wearing a new sling. He and Raciel were taking in everything from liquor to lap dances with economic abandon. Bolan eyed Cuco. He was neither tall nor short, fat nor thin. His graying hair was a brush cut and unkempt, as was his mustache. His suit was cut cheaply, and he wore thick glasses with thick black plastic frames. Cuco Juanmanuel was nondescript to the point of being a cipher. The single vodka martini he'd ordered sat untouched by his left hand. His right hand was out of sight beneath the table. Nacho and Raciel elbowed him from time to time and cajoled him to enjoy himself, but he ignored them. His head slowly swiveled like a surveillance camera, cyclically taking in everyone and everything in the club. Bolan had watched him behave exactly the same way at Miami Jai-Alai, except there he'd scanned the players on the *frontón* the same way and placed occasional bets.

Cuco was the dangerous one, and that was why the Lion had sent him.

Miami-Dade plainclothes Detective Marcus Mandela Mitchell's eyes moved between the stripper on his lap and Gustolallo and her pair of surgically enhanced dancers. He'd obviously developed a crush on his Puerto Rican counterpart and just as obviously had never made the VIP room at Wahoo's. The detective grinned at Bolan and toasted him with his mostly untouched snifter of brandy. "Yo, man! I dig the way you Justice Department dudes roll!"

Bolan shrugged and took a pull off of his Cuban contraband cigar. It was a stakeout, but appearances had to be kept up. He nodded toward their quarry. "I'm going to make a move!"

"I got your back!" Mitchell nodded.

Bolan eyed the enforcer below. "Cuco's the one to watch! Be on guard!"

"Yeah! I feel ya! His shit's been freaking me out all week! Then you fax me that file that he's a *La Neta* assassin. Man, I look at him and feel him in my bones! That four-eyed fuck is a sociopath! Bad medicine! You can read it in his every move!"

The Miami-Dade detective had good instincts. Bolan leaned over. "You're right, and when I make my move, you keep your eyes on him. Nacho's a coward. Raciel is a bully. But Cuco's got the gift of emptiness. Depending on the situation, he may charge down the barrel of a gun. If he does, you drop the hammer on him, and don't stop shooting until he falls."

Mitchell chewed his bottom lip. "Make your move. I got your back."

"Wait a few seconds before coming down and then flank them."

"You got it."

Bolan tucked a twenty into the G-string of the blond stripper blocking his path and rose. Detectives Mitchell and Gustolallo rose behind him. The bouncer nodded and smiled as Bolan and Gustolallo exited. Everyone liked men who brought beautiful women with them to a strip club, and Bolan and his party had tipped well. Bolan felt Cuco's eyes fall on him as he descended the stair. Gustolallo felt it, too. She leaned against Bolan and laughed, and the killer's surveillance passed over them. Bolan got to the bottom of the stairs and Cuco's eyes snapped back and locked on. He saw through Bolan's camouflage and recognized dangerous game.

Nacho and Raciel were clapping their hands and ogling up at the stripper writhing on the pole above their table. Bolan walked straight toward them. Cuco shot an elbow into Raciel's ribs. The leg breaker took one look at Bolan and rose. Nacho looked at Raciel in confusion and then finally caught sight of Bolan. He nearly tipped his chair over backward as he recoiled in horror.

"Fuck!"

"Hey, Nacho," Bolan said. "How's the arm?"

"Fuck you! You're not a cop! You can't—" An ugly gleam of inspiration twinkled in the little man's eyes. "You're not a cop, and that bitch is out of her jurisdiction." He grinned at his bodyguard. "Raciel, break his fucking arm. Break both of them."

The pole dancer screamed and scrambled away from her perch.

Raciel grinned unpleasantly and shrugged out of his coat with practiced ease. He cracked his knuckles and took a step forward. "With pleasure."

Bolan topped Raciel by a head, but the enforcer still out-
weighed the soldier by fifty pounds. Bolan tossed his
whiskey glass to the floor. Raciel's eyes stayed on Bolan's
hands and then he rolled them in contempt as the Executioner cracked his own knuckles.

Bolan spit the whiskey in Raciel's face.

As Raciel blinked and recoiled, Bolan snapped his foot
into the enforcer's groin and he collapsed to the floor,
vomiting. Nacho stared in shock. "Cuco! Do something!"

Cuco rose smoothly from his chair, his hand reaching
behind his back.

Mitchell roared from behind him. "Freeze, motherfucker!"

Cuco froze but his eyes never left Bolan. Mitchell ripped
a .45 Government Model pistol from Cuco's holster then
took a step back with the confiscated weapon. "Now you
just stay real still while—"

Cuco moved.

Most people who survived an encounter with Mack
Bolan had a standard mantra to describe him. The most
common was "scary." A close second was "fast." Bolan
knew in an instant he was facing a killer a full step faster
than he was.

The knife appeared in Cuco's hand like a magic trick,
and he snapped it open in the same movement. He slashed
backward without looking. Mitchell gasped in shock. The
confiscated pistol fell as he slapped his hand to his
bleeding neck.

"Freeze!" Gustolallo shouted. She clawed for her pistol,
but Cuco had already slid to one side to put Bolan in the
line of fire. Bolan knew he'd never clear the Beretta from
his shoulder rig and didn't try. Cuco came for him as fast
as thought. His eyes as flat, black and dead as a shark's as
he came in for the kill.

Bolan stiffened his left hand into a blunt ax and feinted for Cuco's throat. He dropped his hand at the last second, but Cuco was quicker. His downward slash parted the sleeve of Bolan's leather jacket like butter, and the razor-sharp steel opened up Bolan's forearm just below his elbow. Most human beings contracted and froze when cut, but the soldier moved into Cuco's whirlwind of steel. He flung himself into a flying tackle, and the two men flew across the table. The back of Cuco's head and neck slammed into the brass dancing pole with a sickening crunch. His left leg went into convulsions while the rest of his body went limp. Cuco's killing days were over.

Bolan reared up as Nacho tried to draw a Ruger 9 mm pistol. The Executioner slapped the pistol away, and blood flew from Nacho's broken nose as he was backhanded into his chair. "Gustolallo! Help Mitchell!"

Gustolallo vaulted Nacho's table and pressed her hands on top of Mitchell's. "It's bad!"

Bolan drew his Beretta. Raciel was still clutching his crotch, but he had managed to lever himself onto his knees. Bolan drove the butt of the Beretta into Raciel's kidney, which curled him back down into a fetal ball of agony. The Executioner glanced at his slashed left elbow and glared frostily at Nacho, pointing the Beretta between the punk's eyes. "Now I'm pissed."

"Jesus! God! No!"

"You think you can try and kill me and then go on vacation, Nacho?" Bolan loomed over the little man. "You thought I wouldn't come for you?"

"Jesus—"

"Isn't going to help your narrow ass. Now you're going to tell me something. Something good enough to keep me from killing you."

Raciel gasped from the floor. "Give him…nothing! Tell him—"

Bolan cut off Raciel by burying his boot into the man's guts. "Nacho, you'd better tell me something. Raciel here is guilty of assault, and Cuco left a Miami detective with his throat half-cut. No one's going to weep if the Lion's useless little brother isn't brought in alive."

"There've been strangers! There've been—"

Raciel heaved himself to his feet in a remarkable display of loyalty and testicular fortitude. "Nacho, shut the fuck up!"

Raciel's fragile fortitude failed as Bolan's boot took him below the belt for the second time. The enforcer fell back to the floor. Sirens wailed outside. Bolan leveled the Beretta between Nacho's eyes. "Tell me about these strangers."

"Th-they…" Nacho stuttered in terror.

Bolan pressed the selector switch on his Beretta 93-R to three-round-burst mode. "I'm going to count to three."

"I—" Nacho gaped.

"One," Bolan stated.

"But…"

"Two."

"They're not Puerto Rican!" Nacho squealed.

Bolan cocked his head slightly. "They spoke Spanish?"

"Yes!" Nacho shuddered at the enormity of his betrayal. He went from the bedsheet-white of terror to a sickly green. He looked like he might vomit at his own cowardice.

"Cuban?" Bolan inquired.

"N-n-no." Nacho blinked in sick, terrorized confusion. "I mean—I don't think so!"

Bolan eyed Nacho critically. "What did they speak?" Bolan tripped off South American dialects. "Highland Spanish? Lowland? Castellano Argentino?"

"I don't know! They weren't Puerto Ricans! That's all I know! I—"

Miami uniformed police spilled through the club doors with their guns drawn. The point man shouted, "Freeze!"

Nacho sagged with relief.

6

"Hey, Blue, how's the arm?" Detective Gustolallo was leaning against her hotel-room door as Bolan came out of the elevator. He was still wearing a bloodstained T-shirt and his soft body armor. He'd spent the last few hours having pointed conversations with various echelons of the Miami law enforcement community. Many of them weren't happy with his methods.

Bolan held up his bandaged left forearm. "Seven staples. No tendons or nerves cut. Got lucky."

Gustolallo's brow furrowed with sudden concern. "How's Mitchell?"

"He's going to be all right, but he did have tendons, arteries and nerves cut. Cuco went deep on him. He's going to have take some R and R and then have a couple months of physical therapy before he's back out on the street."

"How's he taking it?" she asked.

"When I went to visit him, he was already bragging about how his scar is going to scare the hell out of suspects."

"Speaking of suspects—" the Puerto Rican vice cop's lip curled in contempt "—what about Nacho and his little buddies?"

Bolan had gotten the report from Miami-Dade. "Barring a breakthrough in medical science, Cuco's going to be driving a wheelchair with his tongue for the rest of his life. His cervical vertebrae shattered when he hit the pole."

"Couldn't have happened to a nicer guy."

"Raciel will probably be peeing blood for a week, but he'll live. I made Nacho a little uglier, but he wasn't exactly easy on the eyes to start with."

Gustolallo laughed. "So where're they now?"

"No one's sticking around to press charges. Surveillance says Nacho and Raciel changed their plane tickets for the first flight out tomorrow," Bolan said.

She was appalled. "They're just leaving Cuco behind? Crippled? Cowardly bastards!"

"Yeah, well, Cuco still needs a whole lot of medical attention. The FBI is going to make him an offer in the morning."

Gustolallo chewed that over. "Think he'll turn?"

"Ordinarily I'd say a blank-slate guy like that would never break, but being crippled can do funny things to a man, even if he's kind of funny already. Yotuel's going to know that, too, and you're right, they're throwing him to the dogs. Unless Cuco takes the deal and gets witness-relocated to a private facility and fast, I doubt he's going to live very long."

Gustolallo nodded. "So what's our next move?"

"We're going to the hospital tomorrow. I've arranged a private audience with Cuco before the FBI shows up. I'm going to offer him a straight-up deal he'd be insane to refuse and try to find out what he knows. If he clams up, so be it. We let the FBI take their shot with him and then you and I head back to Puerto Rico and we try to make something happen."

Gustolallo ran her eyes up and down Bolan's frame. "And until then…?"

"Until then I need to get some z's." Bolan eyes roved against his will over Gustolallo's form. He raised his bandaged elbow. "And recover a little blood volume."

The detective giggled and turned her back on him.

"Well, you go recover and I'll go drink rum and read the Bible." She glanced back over her shoulder as she kicked the door shut behind her. "Your loss."

Bolan grinned ruefully and went to his room. He'd been in two brawls and two firefights in forty-eight hours and had gotten zero sleep except for what he had snatched on the plane. He needed—

Bolan caught motion out of the corner of his eye as he closed his door. Splinters flew as he ducked, and the ax was imbedded in the door frame at head level. The figure loomed over Bolan in the darkened room. Bolan grabbed his Beretta 93-R and sprayed three rounds of 9 mm hollow-point ammunition into his opponent. The dark figure was undeterred. The ax was ripped free and it hissed through the air. Bolan felt the cold burn of steel as Kevlar and flesh parted across his chest, but the wound wasn't deep enough into the muscle to affect his aim. Bolan raised the glowing dot of his front sight for a head shot and the pistol drilled another three rounds into his opponent's face. Bolan was mildly surprised to see sparks fly around the dim bulk of his assassin's head.

His attacker was wearing both body armor and a helmet with a ballistic face mask. Bolan took a step back as the razor-sharp edge cut the air inches from his nose. He met the wall of the foyer and slapped the wall switch. Light flooded the room.

The man was clad in a full motorcycle suit and a full-visored helmet. He looked like any one of the thousands of motorcycle enthusiasts who sent their racing bikes screaming through the dangerously curving mountain roads of Puerto Rico. Only rather than racing leather, the assassin was wearing ballistic Kevlar and his helmet had been designed to stop bullets rather than pavement. He also topped Bolan by four inches and in his right hand he held a black iron ax that dripped Bolan's own blood onto the tiles of the entryway. The Executioner was armed with a 9 mm pistol, and his back was against the wall—not quite head to foot.

The ax cocked back for the kill. Bolan snapped his aim down and dumped three rounds into the top of the killer's right boot. The eyes behind the cracked and lead-smeared visor went wide and a muffled roar of shock and outrage vibrated out of the helmet. The ax wavered as the man tottered. Bolan slammed his palm beneath the chin of the helmet and then rammed the muzzle of the Beretta beneath the man's chin. The 93-R cycled another burst.

The assassin went boneless and collapsed to the tiles. The door crashed open beneath Gustolallo's foot. She was dressed only in a hotel bathrobe, and she swept the foyer with her Glock held in both hands. She took in the big man on the floor and the blood all over the foyer with a smirk. "Can't leave you alone for a second, Blue."

"Watch the hall." Bolan quickly swept the hotel suite but his assassin had come alone. "Clear."

Gustolallo closed the door and knelt beside Bolan's assailant. She removed the helmet to reveal a large Latino male with a shaved head. His eyes were crossed and his pupils blown from the bullet's passage through his brain. "He's dead, all right."

Bolan pressed a hand towel against his bleeding chest. "Anyone you recognize?"

"No." She shook her head. "But he's a big mother."

Bolan peered at the ax on the floor. The double-headed blade was black iron, and the socket was dimpled in a patterns reminiscent of West African tribal scarring Bolan had seen in the past. Gustolallo saw where he was looking. "You were talking about axes before."

"Yeah."

"So what do you think?"

"I think the Lion put his little brother out as bait." Bolan nodded at the corpse. "And I think we've met our first *Orisha* headhunter."

"Okay, you know something, Blue?"

Bolan sighed and leaned against the wall. "What's that?"

"Me and you are sharing a room. This shit is creeping me out."

Bolan bled through the towel and went to fetch another one. "That's not a bad idea."

BOLAN GROANED, ROLLED OVER and answered the phone. "Yeah, Bear."

"I hate to ruin your day."

Bolan looked over at Gustolallo's naked form as the sun's rays through the curtains colored her flesh pink, and found it hard to imagine anything ruining his day. "Take your best shot."

"Cuco's dead."

"Something I did to him?" Bolan asked.

"No, you just left him paralyzed. A .32-caliber bullet through the brain last night put him down easy."

"Well, just…crap."

"Yeah, and unfortunately the two cops who'd been stationed outside his door got the same," Kurtzman confirmed. "It was a professional hit."

"Let me guess." Bolan saw where this was going. "No one in the intensive care wing saw or heard anything until Cuco's heart monitor flatlined."

"That's about the size of it. Whoever did it was a ghost, and in Cuco's league of leaving no clues." Kurtzman paused. "You want more bad news?"

"You got nothing on my midnight battle-ax buddy?" Bolan said.

"Um…yeah," Kurtzman admitted. "U.S. and Interpol sources have nothing on him. Fingerprints? Dental? Nada. This guy's a ghost, as well."

"No." Bolan glanced at the iron ax on the nightstand. "He's an *Orisha*. Just like whoever did Cuco in the ICU."

"You're saying he's one of these spirits of vengeance?"

"I'm saying he's an assassin. He's one of our head takers, and he's not an American citizen. I'm not buying the *La Neta* gang, the *Los Macheteros* separatists or even the Puerto Rican drug cartels having hit men with full-on bulletproof motorcycle suits and helmets in inventory. This stinks of foreign intervention."

"Okay, so who's doing the intervening? And is it political or criminal?"

"Don't know yet. Maybe both." Bolan shook his head. "What have you got me on the ax?"

"I ran the photos you sent me against catalog photos in Puerto Rican museums. And there we have some good news. Artifacts like that are generally catalogued and photographed, and even little museums in the Puerto Rican highlands have their own Web sites and online artifact logs to help fellow researchers around the globe."

"So the ax was stolen?"

"No." Kurtzman paused slyly. "According to Puerto Rico's African culture museum's Web site, you can go look at it in the display case right now."

Bolan brought a hand to the painful itch on his chest. "I've got another seven surgical staples that say different."

"So, you're heading back, then?" Kurtzman asked.

"Yeah. I got nothing here. What time does the museum open?"

"Ten o'clock in the morning. You've got a couple hours but it's in the town of Caguas up in the mountains. Barb's arranging a plane and a car for you as we speak."

"How's the rest of my team doing?"

"Well, Ordones and Roldan are currently wanted for questioning by their superiors. They're laying low at a CIA safehouse Barb arranged. Inspector Constante has been put on administrative leave pending an investigation into his actions."

"He's not at the safehouse, is he?" Bolan already knew the answer by the tone of the man's voice.

"No." Kurtzman sighed. "He's wandering around, in broad daylight and dark of night, in the absolute worst parts of town, letting everyone know he kicked *La Neta's* ass. He's saying the gangs are the ones who are traitors to their island and daring them to come out and fight."

"I'll call him and have him meet up with us at the museum. He's tough, but he shouldn't be operating alone. Meantime, see if you can find out anything about the origin of that body armor the assassin was wearing. That was a custom piece, and it was expensive."

"I'm on it." Kurtmann clicked off the line.

Bolan rolled over and prodded Gustolallo with his elbow. "Hey, Juice. You want to go to Puerto Rico's museum of African culture?"

Gustolallo mumbled out of her pillow. "I want pancakes…."

7

Puerto Rico's African Culture Museum

Bolan slowly walked along the wall, gazing at the extended mural that started with idyllic tribal life in Africa and then panel by panel depicted the horrors of capture and detention in the slave forts on the coast, to the even more horrifying transatlantic journey by slave ship to the New World, then to the forced labor on the Spanish plantations and ending with joyous celebrations of freedom. The hall was filled with display cases of tribal artifacts from Africa and their indigenous equivalents made by Puerto Ricans with African ancestry throughout the ages.

Detective Gustolallo leaned against a display case, smoking next to a sign that read No Smoking in two languages, and appeared absolutely bored out of her mind. Bolan idly wandered back to the reception desk. The receptionist on duty was a heavy-hipped, heavy-breasted, broad-shouldered, angry graduate-student type whose riot of curling hair was restrained by a red beret with a gold star. She wore a Che Guevara T-shirt, and her name tag read Juanita. She stared in wary disdain at Bolan over her wire-rimmed glasses. *"Sí?"*

"Is the curator here?"

She spoke her English in clipped tones as if each word of the conqueror's language was a personal injury she was doing to her own honor. "Professor Malibran is very busy, *señor.* May I ask the nature of your business?"

"Oh, well." Bolan shrugged. "My name is Professor Matthew Cooper. I'm with the University of California Berkeley. I'm writing a paper on West African smelting methods. I was doing research in the museums of San Juan when I heard of some of the artifacts you had here. On the mainland we've had some very fascinating recent finds in Georgia and Florida that imply African-American blacksmiths have continued producing artisanal African ironwork among themselves for many generations, some even to this day. We believe this has been paralleled in Puerto Rico, and I would love to compare our finds with those here on your island."

Gustolallo stared at Bolan in awe.

Juanita instantly warmed. "If you will wait, I will fetch the professor." She inclined her head toward an urn on a hotplate behind her. "There is coffee if you wish it."

Bolan grinned like an idiot. *"Muchas gracias."*

Juanita beamed and put a wiggle in her walk for his benefit as she went to the administration wing.

The receptionist returned a few moments later with the professor. He wore his revolutionary leanings on his sleeve, right down to the beret, turtleneck sweater and patchy attempt at a mustache and beard. Thick glasses and poor posture ruined the Che chic he had adopted. "Professor…Cooper, is it?"

"Yes, Professor, and thank you for seeing me on such short notice. I know you must be very busy."

"Not at all, never too busy for a fellow colleague." The professor radiated the fact that he was too busy. "How may I be of assistance?"

"I'm investigating the patrimony of an artifact found in the United States."

"Oh?" The professor raised a dubious eyebrow. "Indeed?"

"Yes. Other than the fact that it was found in Florida, one would swear it was manufactured using West African smelting techniques. The odd thing is, according to metallurgists I've consulted, the object can't be more than a hundred years old."

Professor Malibran became interested against his will. "That is indeed most unusual. That would imply—"

"That the children of former African slaves have been practicing their traditional iron-smithing methods into the last century."

The professor's eyes lit with the zeal of an academic on the hunt. "Or…"

"Or that it was stolen." Bolan reached into the open knapsack over his shoulder and drew the ax. "This look familiar to you?"

The professor gaped.

"As I mentioned, I found the artifact in Florida, specifically in room 302 of the Miami Mandarin Oriental Hotel." Bolan held the ax in front of the professor's face so he could see the dried blood. "Someone tried to take my head off with it last night. Someone removed the heads of three Military Police with it last week. Perhaps you heard."

The professor's mouth opened and then shut.

"I believe this ax is part of your West African collection, catalog number PU-36." Bolan leaned in close. "Are you missing anything?"

The professor's lip quivered. "Impossible…inconceivable."

Bolan didn't like what he saw. Professor Malibran

was scared out of his mind, but he had no idea what was going on.

"It…it should be in the case!" Despite Bolan brandishing an ax, the professor scuttled to one of the cases in the corner of the main hall. "It should be here!"

Bolan drew his Beretta 93-R and pointed at the receptionist's face. "Drop the phone."

Juanita froze in place. Unlike the professor, her eyes betrayed everything.

Gustolallo glared over the sights of her Glock. "Drop it."

Juanita merely smiled.

The professor opened the case with a jangle of keys. He pulled out a black iron ax with a wooden handle, but it had a single, chisel headed bit rather than the curved double that Bolan held. "This is not PU-36!"

That was a no-brainer. Bolan kept his eyes and his gun on Juanita. "Who's on the phone?"

Juanita's smile turned psychotic as she slowly extended the cell phone. "Someone who would like to speak to you."

Bolan placed the ax on a case and took the phone. "Yeah?"

A deep voice rumbled over the phone. "That you, Gringo?"

"Yeah, that you, Yotuel?"

"You are a dead man." The phone went dead in Bolan's hand.

"Everybody down!" Bolan shouted.

The machine gun outside slammed into life like doomsday. The wooden walls of the museum were no defense at all against the cigar-sized bullets that passed through them as if they were paper. Glass display cases shattered in explosions of shrapnel shards. Juanita was the only one to have disobeyed Bolan, and she paid for it as a burst from the crew outside sacrificed her to the revolution.

Bolan glanced at the Beretta in his hand. They were definitely outgunned.

The weapon outside suddenly fell silent as it burned up its one-hundred-round belt. The crackle and pop of small-arms fire filled the gap as the machine-gun crew reloaded. Bolan rose to a crouch. It was time to move.

"Everyone! Behind me!" He threw himself down again as he heard an unmistakable sound and the real hell storm began. Six-foot streaks of fire geysered through the hundred machine-gun holes perforating the museum walls. Bolan took in the stink of burning, jellied jet fuel. They were upping the ante from Molotov cocktails.

Somebody had brought along a flamethrower.

The flame didn't burn out. It fell to the floor in burning puddles and droplets and crawled up the walls. Professor Malibran was screaming and Bolan couldn't blame him. Black smoke sheeted up the entire front of the museum. The enemy would be at all the doors, waiting to shoot them as they came out of the burning building. Bolan grabbed the fallen ax with his spare hand. "Professor!"

The professor screamed as his museum burned.

Bolan started crawling forward. "Professor!"

The professor's howling was cut short as Gustolallo slapped the beret off his head with remarkable force. Malibran rubbed his head and looked up at Bolan dazedly. "*¿Que?*"

"You got roof access?"

"What?" The professor stared dumbly for a moment. Gustolallo's hand cocked back to hit him again and the question suddenly computed. "*Sí!* Yes! We have roof access!"

"Lead the way!" Bolan ordered. "Stay low!"

Professor Malibran scuttled like a crab across the floor, still clutching the imposter PU-36 ax as bullets zipped by overhead. They crawled into the relative quiet of the museum laboratory. Bolan saw the hatch to the attic above and waited for the machine gunner to run dry.

"Now!" Bolan leaped up onto a laboratory bench and caught the knob. He jumped down and the hatch opened. The sliding ladder cascaded down in a clatter, but Bolan doubted anyone outside heard it over the roar of weapons. He ushered Gustolallo and the professor upward. The machine gun roared back into action once more and the rungs beneath Bolan's boots were shot away in the onslaught. He hauled himself up. The attic was filling with choking black smoke, and the wall nearest the front of the building was glowing. Gustolallo stood on a crate to reach the skylight and yanked at the padlock. "Keys, Professor! Keys!"

The professor fumbled through his pockets.

Bolan aimed his Beretta. "Cover your face!"

Gustolallo covered her face as the Beretta barked. The padlock snapped open and spun on its loop with the impact. She unhooked it and slid open the skylight. Smoke updrafted around them in asphyxiating curtains but the promise of fresh air was there. Bolan boosted Gustolallo through the skylight and between them they manhandled Professor Malibran up into the light. Bolan tossed his pistol through the square of blue, then pulled himself onto the roof. "Stay low."

A ten-foot wall of flame and smoke barred their path to the front. Gunshots boxed the compass around the museum. Bolan reached into his shoulder holster and took out the Beretta's skeleton steel folding stock and clicked it into place. He screwed on the suppressor tube and peered over the edge of the museum. He counted about twenty men on foot with small arms and a driver and two crewmen in the jeep with the mounted machine gun. Everyone was in civilian clothing though the jeep was clearly ex-U.S. military.

The person manning the flamethrower, accompanied by a pair of men with submachine guns, was ambling toward the back of the building. All three were smoking and laughing. The level of stupidity it took to smoke while operating a flamethrower had to be regarded with awe. Bolan lined up his sights on the flamethrower operator as he passed by.

The flamethrower pack consisted of two cylinders like a scuba diver's tanks with a compressor tank below them. Bolan lowered his aim slightly for the compressor tank and squeezed the trigger. Sparks flew as the first bullet hit the compressor. Bolan shot the second two rounds into the port fuel cylinder. Compressed fuel squirted. The cigarette fell from the flamethrower man's lips in shock. There was a sound like the slap and whoosh of an ocean wave hitting a cliff, and the three killers disappeared in an expanding ball of fire. Bolan lunged backward as a hot wind reeking of fuel and burning flesh gusted across the roof. Black smoke plumed into the sky, and the men below shouted in alarm. The jeep ground into gear with the .50-caliber machine gun still hammering the side of the museum.

Bolan resumed his rifleman's crouch, peering through the Beretta's sights and waiting for his ride.

He didn't have long to wait. The jeep came fishtailing around the corner, tearing up turf as the gunner continued to fire wildly into the museum. Bolan put three rounds into the driver. The jeep slewed, and the gunner and his mate held on to their weapon for dear life. Bolan shot the gunner, and he toppled off the back as the jeep swerved. The gunner's mate suddenly found himself in a ghost-riding vehicle and threw himself off. The jeep crunched to a stop against the wall of the museum.

Bolan took three running steps and plunged through

space, the hood of the jeep buckling underneath his boots. He rolled off the hood and landed on his feet. "Gustolallo! Help the professor down!"

Gustolallo took Malibran by the wrists and gritted her teeth as she took his full weight and dropped him. Malibran yelped as he fell to the hood. He stared up dazedly and then yelped again as Gustolallo plummeted off the roof, her shoes landing on either side of his head. "Gustolallo! Drive!" Bolan yelled over the sound of the machine gun.

Gustolallo rolled the professor off the hood and pulled the dead driver out of his seat. She gunned the engine into life and crunched the gears as she slammed it into Reverse. "Professor! Get in!"

The professor clambered up gingerly into the blood-spattered passenger seat and nearly fell out as Gustolallo stomped on the gas. "Which way?"

Bolan pointed at the wall of flame. "Punch it!"

Gustolallo punched it. Bolan closed his eyes and the professor screamed as they passed through the curtains of flame. There wasn't much behind the museum besides a small loading dock and tropical forest.

"Which way now?" she shouted

"Turn her around! Right back at them!"

Gustolallo slewed the jeep around in the gravel. Bolan flipped open the feed cover of the machine gun and used the brief moment to lock another belt box of ammo into place. He racked the action on a fresh round. "Right down their throats!"

The jeep plunged through the flames once more.

The men on the other side were already charging the other way, thinking that the jeep had gone around the back. They turned around, jaws dropping in horror as the Fourth Horseman of the Apocalypse bore down on them mounted upon a flaming 4X4. The jeep had picked up burning plasma in its treads. Flame and smoke churned out from the wheel wells like the fiery hooves on an iron hell horse. Bits of burning fuel clung to the vehicle's hood and grille, streaming backward. Bolan held down the trigger and cut loose among the killers. Gustolallo was taking a page out of Inspector Constante's playbook. She drew a line straight through her enemies. Those who couldn't get out of her way were ground down beneath the fiery tires or went flying off the flaming fenders. Bolan and the big .50-caliber weapon claimed any and all who failed to throw down their weapons and cower.

Gustolallo rounded the museum. The front of the building was an inferno. A good dozen men stared in shock as the jeep came around. Bolan wielded the machine gun like a fire hose, and the men who didn't fall scattered. He then riddled a trio of Toyota pickups from stem to stern. The .50-caliber weapon ran dry, and Bolan was out of ammo boxes. "Gustolallo! Get us down the mountain!"

Gustolallo tore out of the tiny parking lot and onto the mountain road.

The right front tire exploded as the flamethrower fuel burned through it and Bolan almost went flying. Gustolallo swore and fishtailed on the melting tires another hundred yards, then both back tires blew like a double-barreled shotgun going off. The left front tire failed, and the jeep sagged and limped fifteen more feet on its rims before grinding to a sparking halt on the narrow road. Gustolallo made several choice remarks in Spanish.

Bolan took up his Beretta and leaped to the asphalt. "Everybody out!" He could hear men yelling and the snarl of at least one damaged engine. "They're coming. Get a little ways down the mountain and then get into the trees."

"No! I'm staying with—"

"Go!" Bolan moved to the side of the road and took cover behind a tree.

Gustolallo grabbed the professor by the arm. "You heard the man! Let's go!"

A bullet-chewed, white Toyota Tacoma came around the bend. Bolan put a burst into the windshield, but the subsonic hollowpoints spalled and smeared across the glass. He changed out magazines and fired again hoping to panic the driver. The obviously experienced driver swerved the truck hard and brought it to a screaming stop so that it took up the whole road. The driver dived out his door, and the half-dozen men in the back leaped out to put the truck body between themselves and Bolan. The Executioner dropped to the ground prone. He reaped a pair of ankles with two three-round bursts beneath the chassis of the Toyota, and when the hobbled men fell, he took their heads. The survivors huddled behind the tires. Two men leaped back for the truck bed. Bolan took out one in midair, but the other made it to safety.

Bolan could hear the rest of the killers running down the road.

The men cowering behind the truck began taking potshots, and Bolan had to duck back as bullets stripped bark off the tree he was using for cover. He shoved in a fresh magazine. Bolan knew he was about to be rushed and vainly wished for a five-gallon bucket of hand grenades.

Bolan's cell phone rang.

He fired a burst around the tree and answered. "Yeah?"

Inspector Constante's voice was jovial. "Sorry we're late, *muchacho!*"

A red Ford Taurus station wagon tore past Bolan's position doing about forty miles per hour and rammed the

Toyota broadside. Several of the men hiding behind it were crushed, while others went flying. Bolan charged. Ordones and Roldan popped out of the back seats brandishing M-16s and shouting orders in Spanish. Most of the gangsters had no choice but to lay where they'd fallen. Bolan came around the crushed cars and paused to stare down at Raciel de Regla, where he sprawled on the pavement. "How's it going, pal?" he asked in Spanish.

Raciel flinched. The leg breaker appeared to have a pair of broken legs himself. His 12-gauge folding stock was out of reach. "Fuck you, white boy."

"You know, murder, extortion, cutting off people's heads? That's all good fun." Bolan glanced over at the museum as it went up in flames and shook his head. "But burning down museums? That's just wrong."

"It's fucked up," Constante agreed, cradling his Thompson. "That's our cultural heritage you torched, my friend."

Raciel peered unhappily between the two men looming above him and seemed to be out of snappy comebacks. Bolan spoke quietly. "Where's Yotuel?"

Raciel glared up at Bolan. "Fuck you, gringo. You better have a blowtorch and pliers, and even then I won't tell you shit. You're a white boy pussy from the mainland. What are you gonna do?"

Bolan considered his subject. He had no doubt he could break Raciel if he had to, but it was something for which he had neither the time nor the inclination. Raciel took his silence for helplessness. "Yeah, that's what I thought."

He flinched as Bolan dropped down into a squat next to him. "You want to know what I'm going to do?"

Raciel maintained a stony silence.

"I'm going to take you to the best hospital in San Juan.

We're going to get you a private room. Get you the best doctor in the joint. Hell, I'm going to keep you there for an extra day so I can fly in a specialist, and I'm going to have steak and lobster delivered to your room daily. I'm going to bring you flowers, personally, and during that time, cops, FBI, DEA, CIA, you name it—you're going to have all kinds of visitors. They're all going to walk in and out smiling."

Raciel paled.

"Your pal Cuco was put down like a dog just to be safe." Bolan locked gazes with Raciel. "What do you think Yotuel and the *Orishas* are going to do when they think you've actually turned state's evidence?"

Raciel knew good and well what Yotuel would do. The details would depend on available time and circumstances, perhaps battery acid, jumper cables and carving knives, or maybe the blowtorch and pliers previously mentioned, but Yotuel would make an example out of him. Raciel's body would end up in the lagoon, and his head would be hurled through his mother's kitchen window.

"You're going to get the best medical treatment money can buy, amigo," Bolan pressed. "The only question is whether you want it in San Juan or in Texas under witness protection."

Raciel's eyes shot pure hatred at Bolan.

"I'm going to count to three." Bolan could smell the fear mixed with rage and frustration boiling in the gangster.

Raciel spit the single word like a curse.

"Texas."

8

CIA Safehouse

"You burned down a museum?" Aaron Kurtzman was incredulous.

Bolan shrugged into the video camera. "It wasn't me."

Kurtzman regarded Bolan sourly. "Then who did burn down the museum?"

Bolan simply said, "People operating flamethrowers shouldn't smoke."

Kurtzman squeezed his eyes shut as he felt a headache coming on.

Kurtzman had absolute faith in Bolan, but the political fallout of the Puerto Rico operation was turning into the proverbial shit storm. Puerto Rico was in many ways almost a separate country, and political goodwill between the United States and its Caribbean commonwealth was failing. Cooperation with local law enforcement had dried up and Inspector Constante, while he still had friends and some cards to play, had officially gone renegade. Vital resources that were needed to help quell the violence were now dedicated to hunting down the inspector and Bolan's team. Oddly enough, the museum massacre was the only faintly positive note. The political wing of the separatists were having a hard time explaining away a bunch of known *La Neta* gangsters burning down a museum devoted to Puerto Rico's cultural heritage.

Bolan considered how literal the "firefight" had been. "The flamethrower still bothers me. Where did they get it? The U.S. military hasn't used flamethrowers since the seventies."

Kurtzman flexed a bit of his encyclopedic knowledge of just about everything. "They also have agricultural uses, Striker. In the U.S. they're used for controlled burns of grasslands. But in Puerto Rico they're used on sugar plantations, and sugar is one of the country's top agricultural exports. There are probably more flamethrowers laying around in Puerto Rico than there are on the entire mainland U.S."

"But our boy wasn't squirting any agricultural propane load. He was using liquid fuel, and it wasn't some backroom brew. The burn was too hot, and I could tell by the stench he was using chemically jelled jet fuel, military grade." Some very ugly memories surfaced in Bolan's mind. "For that matter, Bear, I've been on the giving and receiving end of both the U.S. M2A1-7 and the Russian LPO-50, and our pyromaniac pal wasn't using either one. I didn't recognize the model, and his weapon looked brand spanking new."

Kurtzman grew quiet as he looked into his friend's blue eyes. They had grown glacially cold on the screen. "Most militaries have gone to shoulder-launched rockets to launch incendiaries. There can't be too many culprits. I'll do a search of everyone still manufacturing flamethrowers and get you an illustrated list ASAP. If you can ID the make and model, we'll see if we can find a connecting thread."

"Thanks, Bear." Bolan went on to the next issue. "So how's our buddy Raciel doing?"

"Well, your maneuver paid off."

Bolan hadn't immediately flown Raciel to Texas. He'd let him be taken to a hospital in San Juan. Raciel had received the best medical care available, and Bolan had made sure he'd had surf and turf delivered to his room. A team of federal marshalls would put him in protective custody and take him to an undisclosed location in Texas just as soon as he started talking.

The man sent to interrogate Raciel happened to be Rosario Blancanales. The Able Team warrior was a psychological-warfare expert of the highest caliber.

"I've got Rosario standing by at the hospital with a special Farm laptop," Kurtzman said. "You want to talk to him?"

Bolan punched a key on his own laptop and Blancanales's face appeared in an inset. His wavy hair was slightly disheveled, but his black eyes gleamed with amusement. Bolan could tell the man had come up aces. "Raciel spilled?"

"Oh, he spilled. Not that he had much to tell."

"Anything useful?"

"Well, I think you've got something there with your theory about outsiders throwing fuel on the fire here on the island. Raciel talked about 'strangers' taking meetings with Yotuel and the leaders of *Los Macheteros*. Strangers bearing gifts."

Bolan raised an eyebrow. "Strangers bearing flame-throwers?"

"I don't know about that, but weapons are being funneled in from the outside."

"From where?"

"He said he doesn't know. He said the strangers are definitely not from Puerto Rico. If you can get me one of these strangers alive or intercept a communication I can probably ID him by his accent."

"What else have you got?"

"A lot of names and some locations, but they all involve

La Neta and known members of *Los Macheteros.* Inspector Constante probably knows most of this stuff already."

"All right." Bolan checked his watch. "Keep working him. If you've got nothing by four, give him and everything he's spilled to the FBI, grab our gear from the embassy and meet me at the safehouse."

"I'm on it." Blancanales clicked out.

A window opened on Bolan's screen with a picture of a flamethrower. "That's a Tirrena Model T-148," Kurtzman said. "An Italian job. Look familiar?"

Bolan shook his head. The flame gun was streamlined and modern but the tank assembly only had two cylinders. The weapon used at the museum had been equipped with three. "Nope."

"Hmm." Kurtzman clicked a few keys. "The good news is *modern flamethrower manufacturers* is a pretty short list. How about this one?"

The Italian job disappeared and another inset took its place. It was a perfect match of the one Bolan had blown up. "That's the one."

"Hydroar, LC T1 M-1, made in Brazil. State of the art in flame-weapon technology. It says here it has also been sold to various 'unspecified' armed forces."

"Have Akira hack the Hydroar company database and take a look at its secure sales files. Then see if the Puerto Rican PD was able to pull a serial number off any bits of the weapon that survived the detonation and cross-reference them. See if we can find a point of sale."

"All right. We'll also get those unspecified armed forces specified and I'll have a short list for you in an hour or so."

"Good enough. Striker out."

Bolan closed his laptop as Inspector Constante swept into the room followed by the rest of the team. He grinned at Bolan and lit a cigarette. "Well, we are some very wanted desperados now, amigo."

Ordones laid down a pair of sacks bulging with boxes and foil packages of Puerto Rican takeout and a plastic bucket of beers on ice. "You have good taste." Gustolallo began cracking open beers and the team started tearing into the food.

"So what's next?"

"I have a couple of leads." Bolan packed down plantains. "None of them red hot."

"So." Gustolallo grinned around her beer. "We gonna go make something happen?"

"*Sí,*" Roldan agreed. "We make it happen. That is best."

"It may come to that." Bolan glanced at his phone as it peeped at him. The screen lit up with a tiny aerial photo of the hillside and a schematic of the house. Tiny red lights blinked both above and below the house on the hillside. Someone had breached the perimeter motion sensors on multiple fronts. "Or it may not. Gear up. We're getting hit."

A Squad Automatic Weapon on the hill above them began firing on them. The sliding glass door to the back patio collapsed in a cascade of shattered glass. Bolan snarled. Some of the enemy had broken the perimeter undetected. How the enemy even knew where they were was a question that Bolan would have to go to ask them in person.

"Flaco, take the back. I need you to cover me as I—" Bolan turned as he heard the unmistakable slapping noise of bullets tearing into fabric and flesh. Ordones fell, clutching his groin. Blood squirted between his fingers. He stared up at Bolan in shock. *"Madre de Dios…"*

Gustolallo knelt beside him and flinched as blood sprayed into her face. She turned to Bolan desperately. "It's bad!"

Just by the way he was spraying blood Bolan could tell Ordones had both femoral arteries severed near the source. The grotesque misalignment of his hips told Bolan that Ordones's pelvic bones were broken. "Stick your fingers in the holes!"

Gustolallo gaped in shock. "But, I—"

"Do it!" Bolan yelled.

Bolan caught the sound of M-16s as rifle fire joined the light machine gun outside. He keyed his phone. "Pol! We're under heavy fire! I need medevac and reinforcement now! Make it a Farm priority!" He didn't wait for an answer as he turned to Constante. "Call in! We need immediate extraction or he's going to die!"

Constante got on the phone.

Glass and plaster flew everywhere as the enemy shot the house to pieces. There was no time to wait for the cavalry. Bolan called to Roldan. "You and me! We're going outside! Armor up!" Roldan already has his M-16 in hand, and he yanked his vest out of a duffel. Bolan pulled his Interceptor armor off the corner of the couch and shrugged into it. He picked up Ordones's BAR and flung a bandolier of twelve magazines over his shoulder. Battlefield instincts took over. They had to eliminate the machine gunner and hold the high ground.

Bolan stepped out into the backyard.

The sun was setting and the muzzle flashes of the enemy were lighting up like yellow strobes beneath the thick canopy of tropical trees. Bolan saw the star-shaped fire spray of an M-16 and raised his weapon. He touched off a five-round burst from the ancient iron. The trunks of the thin trees were no cover at all against the machine gun and its steel-jacketed bullets. A man staggered from behind the tree trunk and began tumbling down the hillside.

Bolan raised the BAR and scanned for the machine gunner. But the SAW gunner found him first and a burst of bullets pounded Bolan's chest like a jackhammer and knocked him backward over a lawn chair. Roldan popped off three quick shots, but the machine gunner chased him back through the door with a hail of bullets. Bolan rose. His armor had held, and he had the machine gunner's position cold. He blasted out the remaining fifteen rounds in the magazine and the SAW fell silent. Bolan ejected his empty mag and shoved in a fresh one. Roldan's rifle cracked and the offender tumbled from his cover, rolling down the steep hill.

Bolan stalked to the brick barbecue and snapped out the folding legs of the BAR's bipod. He steadied the huge machine rifle on the lid of the grill and began ripping off short bursts. Brick chips cracked and spit from the barbecue as the enemy fired on him, but the enemy had no cover that the BAR couldn't pierce. Bolan burned through four more magazines. Behind him, Roldan was picking his own shots in rapid semiauto.

The exchange ended as Bolan and Roldan ran out of targets.

Bolan kept his finger around the trigger of the BAR as he checked his cell phone. The motion sensors showed no movement. Heat shimmered the air above the barrel of the BAR as Bolan watched and listened for long moments. He heard the thump of rotors coming up the mountainside from San Juan. "Roldan! Keep watch!"

Bolan ran back into the house. Gustolallo was crying and begging Ordones to hold on. Constante was at the front with his Thompson aimed out a shattered window. Bolan knelt beside Ordones. The big man lay in a sea of his own blood and his face was as gray as ash. The Executioner put a hand on his abdomen—it was as stiff as a board as it filled with internal hemorrhaging. Ordones's mouth worked but little more than a gurgle came out. He let out a long sigh and his huge body went slack.

Sergeant Ernesto Ordones was dead.

Bolan shook his head. Gustolallo pulled her fingers from his wounds and rocked back and forth as she wept. Constante shouted from the foyer as the helicopter rotors rattled the house. "Medevac is here!"

A moment later a pair of paramedics rushed into the house. They dropped down beside Ordones, but their faces were grim even before they checked his vitals. Four men in plain clothes stalked into the safehouse. A bald man a few years Constante's senior and clearly in command scowled at the scene. He paled when he saw Ordones lying dead and Gustolallo clutching him with arms bloodied to the shoulder. "I—"

Bolan's voice was as cold as the grave. "We were set up."

The bald man blinked. "What?"

Constante stared down at his dead friend. His eyes glistened with unshed tears. "How?"

"You," Bolan said.

The sudden silence in the room was deafening.

The bald man shook his head.

"Excuse me. My name is Lieutenant Garbiras, you're—"

Bolan kept his eyes on Constante. "Me, Flaco, Roldan and Gustolallo all dropped out of sight after the battle in *La Perla*. You went downtown and were grilled by your superiors."

Inspector Constante stopped just short of pointing his Thompson at Bolan. His eyes went to slits. "My best friend is dead, and you had better be real fucking sure about what you're saying."

Bolan ignored the impending violence radiating out of

the inspector. "Did you ever take your jacket off while your were being grilled?"

Constante showed Bolan his teeth. "No, I did not take off my jacket, and I did not leave any of my baggage unattended. What the fuck are you—"

"Did anyone give you anything?" Bolan was implacable.

"No, no one gave me shit—wait!" Constante suddenly slapped the chest of his jacket and pulled out a pack of Marlboros. "I couldn't find my smokes, and…"

Bolan's tactical knife clicked open as he took the pack of cigarettes and slit the bottom open. The cardboard bottom was doubled, and sandwiched between the layers was a wafer of electrical board. Everyone stared at the tracking device in shock.

Bolan turned the device in his hand. "Who gave you the cigarettes?"

Constante's anger turned cold and ugly. "A dead man. Detective Jorge Unda."

Lieutenant Garbiras cleared his throat. "I am afraid both of you are under arrest. I'm…!" The lieutenant took a wary step back as both Bolan and Constante turned their gaze upon him.

"Lieutenant, we're not coming in with you today," Bolan stated.

"But—"

"You have a problem with that—" Bolan tore a flap from a takeout box and scratched out a number "—you call this number. Call it now if you like."

Garbiras stared the number as if it were a snake.

"I'm going to ask you not to mention we found the tracking device." Bolan continued.

"I—"

"And I'm going to borrow your helicopter." Bolan

ignored the lieutenant's dumbstruck stare and turned to
Roldan. "Roldan, get Gustolallo cleaned up. The inspector and I will meet up with you later."

Roldan nodded and lifted the weeping woman to her feet.

Bolan knelt and placed the transmitter in Ordones's
pocket. Even in death Ordones was going to get one last
shot in on the enemy.

9

Detective Jorge Unda walked swiftly to his car. He was a big man, black with a shaved head, and his tropical silk suit had been expensively tailored to an impressive physique. His skin was dark, but his hooked nose and almond eyes bespoke some Taino blood. He appeared to be in a hurry. Unda stopped abruptly as a voice spoke behind him. "Hey, Jorge," Constante called out. "Can I bum a smoke?"

Unda turned and smiled shakily around his own cigarette as he found himself face-to-face with Constante. "Hey! Noah!" Unda backed up a step and reached into his jacket. "You—" Unda jumped as he backed into something solid.

He bumped into Mack Bolan.

Unda turned and took Bolan's fist in the solar plexus. The Detective's cigarette wavered in his lips as a second blow took him in the teeth and shoved the cigarette to the back of his throat. Unda dropped to his knees and gagged, almost swallowing the burning cigarette. His watering eyes glared murder as he came back up.

Constante had given Bolan the lowdown on Unda during their helicopter ride. Unda lived well beyond the means of a senior detective and was widely rumored to be on the take, but he was popular in his own right for his bravery and generosity with his money. He also had a reputation for toughness. He came up with his fists ready to fight.

Bolan kicked Unda under his guard as he came up, his

heel hammering the detective's solar plexus a second time. The blood drained from Unda's face and he went back to his knees. Bolan's foot lashed out again and he buried the toe of his boot into Unda's guts.

Unda gasped as Bolan slammed the bottom of his fist like a hammer above his left kidney and then groaned as he gave the right kidney the same treatment. The soldier yanked up his adversary's right arm and Unda roared as Bolan rammed his thumb into the man's armpit like a cold chisel. Bolan mercilessly dropped the dead arm and whipped his stiffened hand around in a short chop that hit Unda between his nose and his upper lip. The blows were calculated not to cripple but to induce crippling pain.

Bolan glanced at Constante. "You want a piece?"

"Me? No." Constante grinned and lit another cigarette. "You are doing just fine. All I have for him is the bullet when you are finished." The inspector drew his .45 and flicked off the safety.

Unda flopped gasping onto his back. Bolan squatted on his heels beside him. "You want to live?" Bolan queried.

"Yeah…"

"So, where were you going in such a hurry?"

"To meet…an informant, I—"

"I think we need to start again." Bolan pulled Unda a few inches up off the ground by his hand-painted silk necktie. "You remember how it felt when I thumbed you in the right armpit? Well, when I do it to the left, the nerve impulses shoot straight to the cardiac tissue. I once heard it described as God stepping on your heart wearing golf spikes." Bolan cocked up his thumb. "This is going to hurt a lot—"

"No, no, no, man!" Unda raised the one palsied hand that still functioned. "I was going to meet some people!"

"Who?"

"I don't know names, man! But they pay long green."
Unda's eyes went wide as Constante stood over him with
the .45. But Unda was as tough as his reputation, and he
glared up at the inspector. "And they support the revolution, not like you, Constante. For all your honest-cop
bullshit, you're just a fucking houseboy." He gave Bolan a
meaningful glare. "For the man."

Bolan read Jorge Unda like a book. Ten years ago he
would have been a stone cold berserker for the revolution,
but now he was in his mid-thirties, married with children.
He expected to be paid to lend his services to the revolution. But by the look in his eyes, more than anything Jorge
Unda wanted to live.

Bolan cocked his head. "You're going to take that
meeting, and we're going with you."

"No fucking way am I—"

Bolan rose and nodded to Constante as he started to
walk away. "Shoot him in the face."

Inspector Constante smiled in the way only those who
have truly been betrayed could smile and pointed the
gaping muzzle of his .45 at the bridge of Unda's broken
nose. "*Buenas noches,* amigo."

Unda screamed. "No!"

Unda screamed again and flinched as the hammer fell
on the firing pin with an empty click. The detective shuddered and wept. Constante pulled back the slide on his
pistol and let it ride home on a live round. "Last chance,
traitor. You talk to my friend or you talk to the gun."

Detective Unda stared up the barrel of the man he'd
betrayed. He squeezed his eyes shut and shook his head in
defeated disbelief.

THEY PICKED UP BLANCANALES on the way. Roldan and
Gustolallo drove in a separate car half a mile behind. Blan-

canales rode up front next to Unda and spoke conversationally about the wonders of Puerto Rico and drummed his fingers on the dashboard to the salsa beats coming out of the radio. Unda squirmed and drove the car. Constante sat behind the traitor with his Thompson aimed at the small of his back. Bolan sat in the back and conferenced with Kurtzman through his laptop, subvocalizing through a microphone taped to his throat.

"The guys who hit us at the safehouse were pros, Bear—trained commandos—and they weren't local. Someone is orchestrating a genuine revolution right here on U.S. soil. There's a government behind this."

Kurtzman sighed. "You're thinking Cuba?"

"I'll admit Cuba was on the top of my list." Bolan frowned. "But whoever is doing this is getting awfully chummy with the drug cartels. There's a lot of things you can say about our old buddy in Cuba, but he's always dealt harshly with the narcotics traffickers in Cuba."

"So now you're thinking…" Kurtzman prompted.

"I'm thinking of another South American strongman who likes to wear red shirts and shake his fist off balconies."

"Venezuela." Kurtzman was almost annoyed that he hadn't seen it. "Well, I'll admit it's intriguing. However, most political observers think if he tries anything in the Caribbean it will be against the Dutch possessions right off his coast. They've already made noise about the islands of Aruba, Curacao and Bonaire being part of a 'Greater Venezuela,' enough noise to make the Dutch send down some ships and marines to the Caribbean for saber-rattling and training exercises."

Bolan shook his head. "Venezuela isn't going to go to war with the Netherlands. They know the United States would step in. Plus those are some very wealthy islands.

They make their money on tourism and offshore finance, neither of which are conducive to socialist revolution among the populace."

"So he's going to take a swipe at the United States instead?" Kurtzman grunted in cold bemusement. "That's awfully bold."

"You've got a little man, sitting on a big puddle of oil with delusions of adequacy." Bolan let out a long breath. "That's always a recipe for fun, and actually the more I think about it the more priceless the plan is. There's no war, no invasion, they just stir the pot enough to help the independence faction win. After that? Once Puerto Rico goes independent they're going to stop getting U.S. federal funding. U.S. investors are going to flee the island for fear of Puerto Rico nationalizing all the industries, and the Puerto Rican economy is going to spin right down the toilet."

Kurtzman saw exactly how it would go. "And then Venezuela steps in like a knight on a shining steed, pumping in millions of their oil money and ensuring that the socialists take power and never lose it." He had to admire the gall of it. "A socialist revolution on American soil, and everyone in Caracas keeps their hands clean. Hell, they end up heroes."

Kurtzman chewed his lower lip in thought. "Well, not to rain on your Caribbean conspiracy theory, Striker, but we don't have a shred of proof we can pin on Caracas."

"I'm working on that. Meanwhile, pull together a Venezuelan connection scenario. A who and how and most likely assets."

"I'm on it."

Unda shifted in his seat uncomfortably. "We are getting close."

Constante lit another cigarette. "How do you wish to play it, Coop?"

"You, Roldan and Gustolallo are known, so you're going to come running when things hit the fan." Bolan turned to Blancanales. "They don't know me and you on sight, so we're going to walk right up posing as Puerto Rican vice cops who have joined the revolution and Unda is our ticket in." Unda jumped as Bolan put a hand on his shoulder. "Right?"

Unda muttered something unpleasant in gutter Spanish.

Bolan's fingers vised down until Unda flinched in pain. "Right?"

Unda grimaced. "Right."

Bolan retained his grip. "Unda, I really need you to get your mind right on this one. Inspector Constante gave me his word he wouldn't kill you if you get this right, but if you get it wrong, you are the most hunted man on Earth."

Multiple moral and emotional crises ground gears behind Unda's eyes.

"I'll put it real blunt for you. Puerto Rico just isn't going to fall today. Not on my watch. You're never going to be a cop again, but if you can hold your mud on this one then you can keep the money the Venezuelans gave you, and I'll top it with a nest egg for your retirement."

It took a moment but Unda's eyes flared in his face, but it was in shock rather than guilt. "What the fuck are you talking about?"

Kurtzman was right. They had no proof but Bolan played the card anyway. "Oh, you didn't get the memo? This time next month, all Puerto Rico is going to be wearing red shirts and saluting to the New Bolivarian Revolution. Screw Uncle Sam, the Boricuas are going to be houseboys to the newest Latin American dictator."

"Fuck you!" Unda snarled.

Bolan bored in mercilessly. "Tell me you got at least a

million. Don't tell me you sold out your department, your fellow officers and your homeland for less than seven figures."

Hatred and shame fought across Unda's face.

"So what I'm going to want now is a list of every officer you know who's involved in this."

Unda's jaws flexed.

"Don't worry, betrayal gets easier with practice, and this time you're going to be doing the right thing," Bolan said.

Unda's shoulders sagged and he started to talk. Bolan typed names into the laptop to send to Kurtzman. Constante grew ever more agitated as Unda gave out a seemingly endless stream of names and ranks. "Well, that's about half the department."

It was far from half, but it was bad. At the end of the day Bolan had about three people he could count on in an island gearing up for civil war. Lieutenant Garbiras was the big gamble. If he'd called the number Bolan had given him, he would know that Bolan had support right up to the commander in chief. Bolan didn't know where the lieutenant's loyalties truly lay, but he had read the man's face when he had seen Sergeant Ordones dead and the lieutenant had been shocked. Garbiras had been horrified when he saw the transmitter and knew the cops were setting up cops for the kill in his own department. Garbiras had gone along. He had taken Ordones's body with the transmitter to headquarters. Then he'd taken the transmitter and put it in a holding cell guarded by men he trusted. The rumor had instantly spread throughout the entire department that Constante had been arrested. Anyone monitoring the transmitter would have Constante pinpointed at San Juan PD HQ. Bolan suspected that an in-station hit was already being set up to take down Inspector Constante.

It was a slim edge, and it could be lost at any second,

but for the first time Bolan and his team had the upper hand on the enemy, and they were going on the offensive.

"Any cops going to be at this meet?"

Unda stared out the window in disbelief at what had happened to his world. "I don't know. There weren't last time. I picked up the money and the transmitter and a man taught me how to turn it on once I'd given it to the inspector."

"So you called in and what did they say?" Bolan asked.

"I told them Sergeant Ordones was dead but otherwise the hit had failed."

"And they told you to come in?" Bolan asked.

"Yeah, and—" Unda snarled.

Bolan interrupted him. "If I'm the one who planted the transmitter, Jorge, then I…" Bolan raised an encouraging eyebrow as Unda did the math.

Unda sagged in his seat. "Oh, fuck…"

"That's right. As long as the inspector is alive, you're a liability to the revolution. You know, you're supposed to be a detective, you should be able to figure this stuff out on your own."

Unda shook his head. "So how the hell am I supposed to get you in there? I'm supposed to be coming alone to my assassination."

"Constante is our ticket in. Your friends don't know me." Bolan nodded toward Blancanales. "And they don't know him. You're going to tell them that we're fellow officers and that we have a plan. We think we can get to the inspector. He's going to be given over to FBI custody in the morning, and we know the delivery time and route. But we want money before we spill."

"And if they don't open the door?"

"Then we kick it down." Bolan took out Unda's service pistol and handed it to him. "You're going to need this."

Constante was appalled. "You're giving this traitor a gun?"

"For better or for worse, he just joined the winning team." Bolan cocked his head. "You on the winning team, Unda?"

Unda drove with his knee as he checked the loads in the Glock and holstered it. "Yeah, I'm on the winning team."

"Good, glad to hear it. Everyone gear up." Bolan began checking his gear. "Let's do this."

10

Blancanales had flown straight from the Farm to Puerto Rico and he had brought the candy store with him, including role camouflage. Bolan changed into a decent-looking blue suit that had been tailored to conceal the shoulder rig he wore. They had to pass visual inspection on the walk up, and once inside they needed overwhelming firepower. The weapons for this meet were BXP submachine guns. They fired at a thousand rounds a minute and were probably the only submachine guns in the world that had an attachment for firing grenades.

Blancanles had brought an assortment.

Bolan clicked on his tactical radio so Roldan and Gustolallo could hear in the car behind them. "All right, my associate and I are going to walk straight in with Unda, who is going to do most of the talking. If I have to say more than yes or no in Spanish, our cover is blown. We have no idea of the number or composition of the enemy. We have to assume at least some of the hitters from this morning's operation may be there and heavily armed. They're going to be on a high state of alert. Roldan, I want you to take the BAR and hold the back. The inspector and Gustolallo will deploy once we're in. They'll either plug holes or come in like the cavalry as needed."

Gustolallo and Roldan came back in the affirmative. Bolan and his team waited as Roldan deployed into the trees, weighted down with Ordones's machine gun as well as his own M-16. "In position!" Roldan spoke breathlessly.

Bolan nodded at Unda. "Let's go."

Unda pulled the car up the narrow road and into the drive. Bolan slipped on a pair of shades, pulled on a Panama straw hat and lit a cigarette. As long as he kept his mouth shut, he looked every inch a detective of San Juan Vice. He and Blancanales fell in to formation on either side of Unda as they walked up the gravel drive and into the trap. Behind the suburban Spanish-style house there was a bit of woods that led to a horse ranch and then rolling foothills above. Perfect for insertion and extraction from city to countryside. Bolan subvocalized into the mike taped to his throat. "Roldan, we're going to assume that the *rancho* up the hill has been compromised. If the enemy has reinforcements, they'll be coming your way."

"Roger that, Coop," Roldan answered. "I will be ready."

Bolan waited for the hail of bullets as they walked up to the door and Unda slammed the wrought-iron knocker five times in rapid succession. The door opened almost instantly. A very angry-looking man with a mustache and a cocked .45 in his hand glared at Unda. Two other men with M-16s stood behind him. A rapid exchange of Spanish took place. The gist of it was what in the blue hell was Unda doing bringing strangers to the meet. They stood on the porch on the verge of being cut to pieces as Unda and Blancanales rolled out the big lie.

Blancanales and Unda talked about times, routes, money and the fate of Inspector Constante.

Angry words shot back and forth, but Bolan could read the first thug's body language. He wanted Inspector Constante, he wanted him bad and he was buying the lie.

With Constante on the table Unda had been granted a temporary stay of execution. The man jerked his head for them to enter.

They walked down a dim, tiled hall and came to a large living room where half a dozen men lounged on couches, watching a soccer game on a giant plasma-screen television. Their eyes swiveled to Unda and his party, and Bolan knew these men were not gangsters or even nationalist revolutionaries. Just by the way they lounged it was clear these men were highly trained soldiers and, despite their civilian clothes, it was clear that they were armed, on duty and ready to go into action at a moment's notice.

"If what you say about knowing Constante's route is true, my friend, this is your lucky day," the man with the mustache said.

Blancanales shook his head in disgust. "Constante is a fucking ball-breaker. All day, every day, you have to walk on goddamn eggshells around him." He gave a very Latin shrug. "Fuck him. He had his chance. He's either with us or against us."

The man seemed to accept this without any commitment on his part. He glanced at Bolan. "Who's he?"

Blancanales smiled guilelessly. "Show me some money."

The man nodded at a man who rose and went into a back room. He returned with an aluminum briefcase. He flipped the latches to reveal banded stacks of U.S. one-hundred-dollar bills.

Blancanales gazed at the money admiringly. "Shit…"

The man with the mustache, an apparent leader, nodded at Bolan. "So, who is this asshole?"

"Why—" Blancanales grinned from ear to ear "—he just happens to be the man driving Constante to FBI headquarters tomorrow."

Bolan shrugged in acknowledgment.

The thug's eyes widened. "No shit?"

"No shit," Blancanales confirmed. "You pick your street, any street along the route, and me, my friend here and dear old Inspector Constante will make an unscheduled turn. We'll hand him over to you on a silver platter."

Mustache actually smiled.

Unda nodded eagerly. "I told you I was connected. I know these guys. They're realiable, and we can make this work. You pick the turnoff, and once we turn, you arrange to have the street blocked behind us. After that we hand you Constante alive and unarmed. We find out who this gringo is. We find out who else on the force is working with Constante. We find out everything."

He seemed pleased with everything except Bolan. "Your friend doesn't say much."

Blancanales began ad-libbing fast. "Well, his nickname is Silence. He pretty much just drives and hurts people. That's to your advantage."

The man kept mad-dogging Bolan. "I know I've seen you somewhere, Mr. Silence. Why don't you say something?"

Blancanales sighed. "Listen, amigo. My friend does not do this for the people like the rest of us. He does this for the money. It is of no matter. Like I say. I will give you the time and the route. You pick your street and find a way to shut the door behind us. Silence and I will deliver the inspector as promised. No problem."

Mustache considered that.

A man rose from the couch and Bolan didn't like the way he was looking at him. He leaned into the ear of the man with the mustache and whispered something. The man's seemingly constantly grim expression grew even grimmer. "Silence?"

Bolan grunted noncommitally and shook himself out another cigarette from his pack.

"Canelo says he knows you from someplace," Mustache said. "I think so do I."

Bolan knew the situation was seconds from going out of control. He put his lighter back into his jacket and his hands closed around the grip of the BXP. He glanced out the window facing the courtyard. "Who the hell is that?" he said in Spanish.

Heads turned and Bolan tore open his shoulder holster, setting the BXP free while he spun 360 degrees. He hit both men behind him and continued his turn, aiming the gun at the man's head. Blancanales covered the staggered guards behind them. Unda drew his pistol and aimed at the men on the couch. Bolan spit out his cigarette. "How many more men here in the house?"

Mustache glared down the submachine gun with the conflicted fervor of a revolutionary who has ordered men killed but never faced death himself. The soldiers sat on the couch coldly waiting for the right opportunity to go for their guns. Bolan eyed Mustache. "Just so you know, I'm the gringo."

The man with the mustache paled.

"I'm going to ask you one more time." Bolan nodded. "Then I'm going to give you to Constante. He's just outside and he's very angry about Sergeant Ordones. Unda has already made a deal to keep his balls. I suggest you do the same."

Canela turned his head toward the man with the mustache but his eyes, full of zeal, never looked away from Bolan. "Tell the Yanqui nothing."

Bolan snapped his aim over and shot Canela in the shoulder.

Get FREE BOOKS and a FREE GIFT when you play the...

LAS VEGAS

GAME

*Just scratch off
the gold box with a coin.
Then check below to see
the gifts you get!*

YES! I have scratched off the gold box. Please send me my **2 FREE BOOKS** and **FREE GIFT** for which I qualify. I understand that I am under no obligation to purchase any books as explained on the back of this card.

366 ADL EVMJ　　　　　　　　　　　　　　**166 ADL EVMU**
(GE-LV-09)

FIRST NAME　　　　　　　　　　　　LAST NAME

ADDRESS

APT.#　　　　　　　CITY

STATE/PROV.　　　　　ZIP/POSTAL CODE

7	7	7	**Worth TWO FREE BOOKS plus a FREE Gift!**
🍒	🍒	🍒	**Worth TWO FREE BOOKS!**
🔔	🔔	♣	**TRY AGAIN!**

Offer limited to one per household and not valid to current subscribers of Gold Eagle® books. All orders subject to approval. Please allow 4 to 6 weeks for delivery.

The Gold Eagle Reader Service — Here's how it works:

Accepting your 2 free books and free gift (gift valued at approximately $5.00) places you under no obligation to buy anything. You may keep the books and gift and return the shipping statement marked "cancel." If you do not cancel, about a month later we'll send you 6 additional books and bill you just $31.94* — that's a savings of 15% off the cover price of all 6 books! And there's no extra charge for shipping! You may cancel at any time, but if you choose to continue, every other month we'll send you 6 more books, which you may either purchase at the discount price or return to us and cancel your subscription.

*Terms and prices subject to change without notice. Prices do not include applicable taxes. Sales tax applicable in N.Y. Canadian residents will be charged applicable provincial taxes and GST. Offer not valid in Quebec. Credit or debit balances in a customer's account(s) may be offset by any other outstanding balance owed by or to the customer. Offer available while quantities last.

BUSINESS REPLY MAIL

FIRST-CLASS MAIL   PERMIT NO. 717   BUFFALO, NY

POSTAGE WILL BE PAID BY ADDRESSEE

GOLD EAGLE READER SERVICE
3010 WALDEN AVE
PO BOX 1867
BUFFALO NY 14240-9952

NO POSTAGE
NECESSARY
IF MAILED
IN THE
UNITED STATES

The men on the couch popped up and produced their .45s. The first man up aimed at Mustache, and Bolan burned him down with a burst through the chest. The second one managed to put a bullet between the shoulder blades of Mustache. The revolutionary cried out and fell. Bolan shot the gunner down. Blancanales took down the two guards behind them with a pair of bursts. Unda staggered as he took a bullet in the chest, but his armor held and he hammered down the man who'd shot him. The Executioner put a burst into the last two soldiers and his weapon clacked open on empty. He ejected the magazine and shot the slide home on a fresh one from under his coat.

Voices began shouting throughout the house. Constante's voice came across Bolan's tactical radio. "Cooper! We heard shots! Do you require reinforcements?"

"Not right now. All outside units hold the perimeter." Bolan knelt beside Mustache. The man gasped and wheezed past a collapsed lung. "Belay that. I need you to come in and extract a VIP suspect. He needs medical ASAP."

"Affirmative, Coop," Constante replied. "I am coming in."

Bolan slapped out the folding stock on the BXP. Constante charged in with his Thompson at the ready. He slung his weapon and began applying a field-dressing to the fallen revolutionary. The man groaned as the inspector hooked him under his arms and began dragging him outside. Unda picked up a fallen M-16 rifle. Bolan took point as he began to sweep the house.

Down the hall a pair of .45s began barking. Bolan pulled a hand grenade from his jacket pocket and pulled the pin. The metal cylinder clanked and skipped down the tiled hallway. Bolan heard the horrified shout in Spanish at the other end of the hallway.

The warning shouts were eclipsed by a 170-decibel

thunderclap and the 2.5-million candela lightning flash of
the stun grenade. Bolan charged down the hall through a
firefly cloud of winking orange pyrotechnic aftereffects.
The hall opened to a bedroom on either side. "Pol!" Bolan
ordered. "Go left!" Bolan went right. Two men with pistols
were blinking and yawning and yelling in the aftermath of
the flash-bang grenade. The Executioner drove the steel
strut of the BXP's folding stock into the jaw of one half-
blinded man and sent him to the floor with a shattered
mandible. The second gunner managed to squeeze off a
shot that was high and wide before he took the buttstroke
between the eyes. In the other room Blancanales's weapon
snarled off a long burst. "Pol!"

Blancanales emerged and shook his head. "One hostile
down! Clear!"

"Clear!" Bolan called as he hog-tied the two fallen men
with plastic restraining strips. He looked up as heard the
rapid slamming of the BAR behind the house and called
across the tactical link. "Roldan!"

Roldan shouted back over the radio. "Rabbits running,
Coop! Three down! Three more running back in your way!"

"Roger that!" Bolan strode to the end of the hall and into
a living room followed by Unda and Blancanales. He
kicked out the screen door leading onto the courtyard as
three armed men ran into it. Bolan's and Blancanales's
BXPs buzz-sawed in their hands and the three gunmen
shuddered and fell.

"Pol! Check them! Unda! With me!"

Bolan and Unda swept the rest of the house and found
no more hostiles. The Executioner spoke into his tactical
radio. "House is clear! Inspector, we have two prisoners!
Pol, what's your status?"

"Three KIAs in the courtyard. Linking up with you now."

"Clear! Come ahead."

The BAR out back slammed back into life. "Shit!" Roldan shouted. "I've got company! Coming down from the *rancho!* Heavily armed! Squad strength!"

Bolan broke into a run. "We're coming! Gustolallo! Inspector! Move in!" Bolan broke out the back door. The bit of woods between the house and the *rancho* crackled with high-powered rifle fire.

Bolan knelt behind a tree and raised his weapon to his eye.

Two men charged toward him. Bolan squeezed his trigger and the closest gunner jerked and twitched as the burst took him out. Off to the side, Bolan could hear the short brap-brap-brap of Constante's Thompson and then the second man stumbled. Gustolallo's shotgun slammed once and took the man off his feet and dumped him to the dirt. Bolan shouted, "Roldan! You all right?"

An arm waved over the top of a fallen tree. "I'm okay! They're falling back!"

Blancanales ran up and knelt beside Bolan. "How do you want to play it?"

Bolan spoke into his radio. "All units! We take the *rancho!* Full assault!"

Constante and Gustolallo came running. Roldan rose with the BAR slung in the hip-assault position. Bolan and his team loped through the trees in a loose skirmish line. Through the trees Bolan could see six fleeing men. One was being supported by two of his comrades. They ran across the corral and piled into the barn.

Bolan held up a fist as he reached the edge of the trees, and his team huddled together. "Roldan, same plan. Skirt wide and get behind the barn with the BAR. You've got the back door." Roldan rose without a word and ran wide. Bolan took his two remaining grenades from behind his back. He had a frag and an antiarmor round. "Pol, what have you got in the way of grenades?"

"Well…" Blancanales checked his personal supply. "I've got a frag, a white phosphorous and tear gas."

Roldan called in. "I'm in position. I have a clean line of sight on the back of the barn and most of both sides."

"Roger that." Bolan glanced at the assortment of grenades. "Okay, here's how I want to play it. Pol, I want you to put the tear gas into the barn through the window and then set fire to the roof with the Willy Pete. Inspector, once we hear them hacking and the roof is falling down around their ears I want you to announce yourself and tell them to surrender. They'll have been warned about you and know your reputation. With any luck they might just think they're going to be arrested and if they believe lawyers and bail are involved they might come without a fight."

"Hmm." Constante lit a cigarette. "It's worth a try."

Blancanales clicked the tear-gas grenade into positon on his weapon, adjusted his sight and nodded. "On your go."

"Go," Bolan said.

Blancanales sent the tear gas canister unerringly across the empty space between the barn and the trees to sail through the open hay-winching window in the loft. Then he took up the white-phosporous grenade and reloaded. The top half of a double Dutch door slammed open. Bolan fired off a burst, but not before the interior of the barn lit up in orange light and the football shape of an RPG rocket came spiraling in toward Bolan and his team's position in the trees. Bolan's voice boomed. "Down!"

The RPG hit a tree trunk and the world turned into a concussive, superheated slap of smoke and fire. Shrapnel ripped through the air like a withering wind. Bolan looked up and ducked down again as a LAW rocket hissed and sizzled on the heels of the RPG. An M-60 machine gun blazed into life and chewed holes through the barn door in their general direction as the enemy fired from within. An M-79 grenade launcher blooped pale yellow fire through the same hay window Blancanales had lobbed his gas grenade.

Bolan was beginning to suspect that the barn just might be one of the revolution's weapon depots.

Roldan shouted excitedly across the channel. "What the hell's happening? Is that you or the enemy firing?"

"Roldan! We're taking heavy fire!" The only good news was that the thin board walls of the barn would not stop the heavy 30.06 bullets from a BAR. "Light 'em up! Disperse your fire across the entire structure!"

"*Sí*, Coop! Commencing fire!" The BAR began making a dim counterpoint beneath the roar of Armageddon erupting from the barn's every opening.

Bolan and his team hugged the dirt and any tree available as the enemy cut loose with an array of support weapons.

"Same plan?" Blancanales asked.

"No! They want the thunder, then we'll give it to them!"

Blancanales rose up despite the barrage and fired his weapon through the open Dutch door.

Bolan glanced at Constante. "You okay?"

Constante's face was blackened with smoke. "I'm okay!"

Bolan picked up the inspector's left forefinger from among the leaves and shoved it into the man's breast pocket next to his cigarettes. "You're going to want that later!"

Constante stared at his ragged stump and then looked up with a grin. "Thanks!"

Unda appeared to be bleeding from both arms and his upper back, but it didn't stop him from firing short bursts toward the barn.

The barn doors smashed open and wood flew in all directions as a truck came roaring out of the tear gas and smoke. The 4x4 vehicle had a pair of M-60 machine guns mounted behind a chicken shield in the back. The windshield had been knocked out, and the man in the passenger seat was firing a rifle. Sparks shrieked off the hood as Blancanales, Constante and Unda returned fire and more bullets whined off the gunner's glacis. The twin guns swiveled around and sent swarms of lead tearing through the trees.

Bolan shoved his antiarmor munition over the launch rings. He lead the truck slightly as it shot toward the road and fired. The BXP bucked and the rifle grenade spiraled into the 4x4's right front wheel well. The tire exploded with impact and the warhead detonated. The hood shot skyward on a column of black smoke, and the two men in the cab screamed as superheated gas and molten metal blasted through the vents and seared the interior. The truck skidded as the right fender dropped and plowed earth. The man in the back screamed as the 4x4 tipped over. The screams were cut off when the truck rolled and man and machine gun were mangled into each other. The 4x4 came to a stop on its side where it lay on fire.

The barn was burning like a torch and it shuddered as munitions began exploding within. Bolan and his team stayed hunkered down in the trees as grenades and rockets blew and small-arms ammunition cooked off like popcorn. Black smoke mixed with the gray fog of the tear gas. Bolan kept his sights on the burning building, but no one was coming out. The barn groaned in its death throes and collapsed in upon itself.

11

Private Clinic, Catano

A phone call from the Department of Justice had convinced the clinic administrator not to report the two carloads of shot and wounded people to the local authorities and to close the clinic for the rest of the day. Unda had a dozen cuts but only four or five of them of them had required stitches—he was a very lucky man. The clinic's surgeon had informed Inspector Constante in the strongest terms that if he wanted to save his finger he needed to go to the main hospital in San Juan immediately and keep the hand immobilized for several days.

Constante had responded by taking his severed finger, throwing it in the medical waste bin and telling the surgeon to stitch over the stump.

Inspector Noah Vincente Constante was about as tough as they came.

Roldan was almost embarrassed that he had no battle damage to speak of and sat up on the roof of the clinic with his scoped M-16 keeping an intense watch on the streets.

Bolan went back to the E.R. and examined their suspects. The suspected revolutionary—the man with the mustache—had been stabilized, but he was heavily sedated and wouldn't be available for questioning for hours, perhaps not until the following day. Of the two suspected commandos, one had a shattered jaw and wouldn't be talking at all for weeks. The other had raccoon bruising around his eyes and a lump the size of an egg between his eyebrows. He was definitely suffering from a concussion, and the doctor wanted an MRI to look for splintering or fracture of the skull.

Blancanales walked over and ran a hand through his hair. "You want to have a talk with our concussed amigo, don't you?"

"No, Pol," Bolan said tiredly. "I want you to have a talk with him."

Constante walked over and looked toward the lounge where Unda sat by himself drinking a soda. The detective was wrapped in a number of bloody bandages. He also still had his gun. The inspector's eyes narrowed. "So, what do you think?"

It was an interesting question. "I don't know. What do you think?" Bolan countered.

Constante gazed at the detective in open scorn. "I think Detective Jorge Unda is a corrupt cop. He is a traitor to his department, his fellow officers and the island of his birth."

Bolan nodded. "I'm thinking about offering him a job. How do you feel about that?"

"Cooper…" Constante's voice lowered. "He got Ordones killed."

"Yeah, he was involved. No doubt about it." Bolan raised an eyebrow at the inspector. "The question is, can you work with him?"

Constante awkwardly fished out his pack of smokes, glared at the No Smoking sign on the wall and put them back. "So, what is this, a shot at redemption?"

Blancanales watched Unda as he sat by himself and stared at his sweating can of soda. "I've seen worse cases." He nodded toward Bolan. "And I've seen him redeem them."

Habit overcame reason. Constante lit up a cigarette and took several long drags to buck himself up. He suddenly barked into the lounge. *"Che! Unda!"*

Unda just about jumped out of his bandages. He rushed over but slowed warily when Constante rested a hand on the butt of his .45 and flicked off the safety.

Constante wrinkled his nose like he smelled something unpleasant. "Listen, Jorge. You're dirty. And I want to kill you, but this Yanqui and his friend want to give you a job. You want a job?"

Unda kept his eye on Constante's gun hand.

"You did okay back there, Unda," Bolan said. "You ready to keep rolling with us? You can say no. I'll cut you loose, and you and Constante can work things out when this is over."

"Oh, I will roll with you. I want to roll every one of these *venezolano* motherfuckers into the sea. Tell me what you want me to do."

Bolan had been giving that a great deal of thought. "By now the enemy knows we hit them at the ranch house, but with any luck they still think the inspector is back in a holding cell at headquarters and Unda is still on the payroll. Unda, you're going to make a call and tell them the same story. Constante is being moved to the CIA San Juan station. You're going to give them a time and a route."

Blancanales grimaced. "This is all assuming Garbiras hasn't gotten cold feet and given us up. For that matter the entire place is full of police. It'll be a miracle if one of them hasn't figured out something is wrong. Plus, given the ranch house hit and all the losses they've taken, you think they'll stick their neck out just to nail Constante?"

"I hear you," Bolan agreed. "But Unda's going to make two calls, one that Constante is going to the CIA station, and then another more urgent one that I'm going to be in the car with him. We'll see who bites at that."

Blancanales still didn't like it. "What if they decide taking the both of you alive is too risky and they decide to light you up instead? And even if we pull a switch and you and the inspector aren't in the car, it's a suicide mission for whoever's driving decoy. We can't ask anyone to do that."

Gustolallo called out, "I'll do it! So will Roldan!"

"No." Bolan shook his head. "I'll be driving, and with me, Constante and Unda. They want us alive. They want answers."

Bolan looked from Constante to Unda. "Well, you've heard my plan. You in?"

Constante held up his maimed hand. "I would love to go for a romantic car ride with you, my friend."

Unda simply said, "I'm in."

Bolan nodded. "All right. Make the call."

BOLAN'S TEAM SAT IN the holding cell. Despite having a concussion, their prisoner had kept his teeth clenched and said nothing. The doctor had warned Bolan that anything more strenuous than threats could kill him. Bolan stared at a map of downtown San Juan that lay on the table before them. They were going to have to make their run without much in the way of intelligence on their enemy's numbers or disposition. Bolan turned to Unda. "What have you got?"

"I made both calls, like you said. Both times a voice I didn't know thanked me for the information and hung up before a trace could be started." Unda pointed a finger skyward. "But I put a few calls in to informants I have on the street. The most interesting thing I learned is that a call has gone out to the rent-a-mob circles, and there's going to be a student riot during Inspector Constante's scheduled ride."

"Really?" Bolan found the timing intriguing. "Where?"

Unda stabbed a finger onto the map. "Right here—in the middle of our route." He traced the cross street. "You are going to be forced to turn right if you wish to proceed to the CIA station."

Bolan admired the trap. "The mob will force us to turn and then fill in the street behind us. Unless we're willing to run down college students we'll have no back door. They'll pull a pin, point RPGs, and if Constante's car doesn't surrender immediately, they'll blow it sky high."

Bolan turned to Constante. "What does Garbiras have to say?"

The inspector did not look pleased. "He asked for volunteers to reinforce the convoy, but no one is stepping up. He had to order men to take the lead and tail cars. They won't assist in taking us down, but none can be relied upon to aid us, either."

Bolan looked over their route and the diversion a final time. "All right, it's going to go like this. Constante and Unda are going to be in the target car."

"And me!" Gustolallo insisted. "I'm in that car. Don't even think of telling me I'm not."

"You're going to be riding shotgun, literally. Load your gun with slugs. I want full penetration on windshields and car doors."

"You got it," Gustalallo said.

Gesturing to Blancanales, Bolan said, "We'll be shadowing the convoy on motorcycles and should be able to weave through the rioters or go up on the sidewalk."

Roldan peered at the road map on the table. "And me?"

"Last time I heard you made marksman with that rifle of yours, and Garbiras says the chopper is all ours." Bolan pointed a finger skyward. "I want you pulling guardian angel duty and coordinate us from up top. You down with that?"

Roldan nodded. "Oh, I'm down with it."

Bolan looked around his team. "Questions?"

Unda slapped the pistol holstered on his belt. "I would like something a little bigger."

Bolan shrugged. "What else have you qualified with?"

"We used Uzis when I was on the stakeout squad."

"The inspector will make that happen. Everyone else?" Bolan checked his watch. "We are go in one hour, fifteen minutes and counting. Once you've got your gear squared away I suggest you grab a nap or drink yourself one whole hell of a lot coffee. It's going to be a very interesting afternoon."

12

The convoy consisted of two unmarked Chevy Impalas front and back and a Chevy Suburban that Unda was driving in the middle. Bolan hung back on his BMW Dakar motorcycle. Blancanales had acquired himself a Harley Shovelhead.

Bolan spoke into the radio on the team's private frequency. "Roldan, how does it look ahead?"

The helicopter was pulling a high and wide orbit over central San Juan. "Looks like Unda's intelligence was gold," Roldan came back. "Ten blocks up, south of the university, you got a crowd gathering—signs, people with bullhorns, guitars, flowers and flags, the whole bit—and it is getting larger by the second. Hundreds of civilians are in the crowd."

"Roger that, Roldan." Bolan said. "All units, you heard him. We can afford zero collateral damage. Repeat, zero collateral damage."

Everyone came back in the affirmative. The convoy moved up another block, but it was already slowing when Bolan glanced up at the sky as plumes of black smoke began to rise through the shimmering heat. "Roldan, I have smoke ahead."

"People are lighting fires in trash cans," Roldan responded. "Be advised uniformed police units are beginning to arrive on the scene."

Constante's job at the moment was monitoring the police band, and he broke in. "Be advised, crowd control has been mobilized."

"Be advised," Roldan added, "a car was just turned over and set on fire. Individuals in the crowd have incendiaries. Looks like Molotov cocktails, can't be sure."

The convoy proceded forward another few blocks. More smoke was rising in thick plumes over San Juan, and Bolan could hear the chanting and the bullhorns over the sound of his motorcycle's engine. Bolan could feel the anger in the air. His instincts spoke to him.

"Listen up, I think this is going to be a hit, and it's going to happen right in the middle of the riot, where a burned car full of cops will be just another national tragedy, civilian casualties will feed the fire and Constante's death will be a lesson to the rest of the police on the force."

"Do we abort?" Unda asked.

"No." Bolan had made his decision. "We go right down their throats. Roldan, what's the status on police presence?"

"They've formed a skirmish line on the northern side of the protest, but they're looking thin on numbers."

Bolan knew little help would be received from the local police.

The convoy was moving west to east. "How about on the south and west sides?"

Roldan's voice was grim. "No visible police presence from the air."

The situation was clear. When they hit the crowd, it was going to be a free-for-all. "Pol, when we get close, you and I are going to run interference for Unda."

Bolan opened one of his saddlebags to reveal a pack of rifle grenades sticking up butt first. Bolan drew his BXP from the shoulder rig beneath his jacket and shoved the muzzle of the weapon into the base of one of the grenades until the launching rings clicked into place, then glanced over to see Blancanales doing the same. They gunned their bikes forward and moved past the police convoy, keeping their weapons half under their jackets. "We fire at one hundred yards, overhead and into the crowd," Bolan said.

Blancanales glanced over and pulled an old-fashioned pair of biker goggles over his eyes. "Definitely should have worn a helmet."

The convoy continued toward the growing maelstrom of angry humanity. Bolan could just see people running back and forth in the distance. Glass shattered as someone hurled a newspaper dispenser through a shop window and people began looting.

"I'm calling it a hundred yards," Blancanales said.

Bolan slapped down the folding stock of his weapon and put it to his shoulder. He and Blancanales fired simultaneously. The BXPs sent their payload spiraling above traffic toward the seething crowd. They fired again and then gunned their engines, weaving their bikes through the remaining traffic. Bolan swerved around a delivery van, and people screamed and dived out of the way as he drove up onto the sidewalk.

The gray mist of tear gas began mixing with the black smoke of burning vehicles and the fires set in trash cans.

Unda's radio crackled. "Our caravan guards saw you fire. They want to know who the hell you are and what you're doing. You want me to tell them you're with us?"

"No, tell them they're with me and they'd better decide right now if they want to do their job or bug out. If they betray us once when we hit the riot, I'll blow them straight to hell."

"Madre de Dios…" Unda was shocked, but Bolan's message went out in Spanish over the open channel.

Bolan and Pol continued on. "Roldan, what have you got up top?"

Roldan laughed. "People on the police band are screaming. Everyone wants to know who fired gas. Units on the north side of the disturbance have begun firing their own tear gas into the crowd just because you did. If it wasn't a riot before it is now."

They'd caught a break. Bolan and Blancanales couldn't blanket an entire city block with their weapons, but with the San Juan PD unwittingly helping out they just might be able to win their way through. The gas would disperse all but the most hard-core rioters. The assassins would stay the course.

Then Unda's voice came over the secure channel. "*Putos!* Cooper! We just lost our lead car!"

Bolan turned to see the San Juan unmarked Impala making a hard right and peeling away at high speed. "Forget them! Keep moving forward!" Bolan slapped down his helmet's visor. It would buy him a little time from the effects of the gas, but he could already smell its acrid stink. He gave the bike some gas and rolled straight down the middle of the riot to the next block. A thrown rock hit him in the chest and an egg slopped across his shoulder, but revving his engine and brandishing the BXP made most people get out of his way. Blancanales rolled in flanking position on the other side of the avenue.

The Suburban rolled into the riot and attracted a hail of rocks, bottles and eggs. A surge of young men charged the vehicle and began rocking it back and forth, trying to roll it. The front and back windows rolled down just enough to drop a pair of grenades on either side. The four Sting Ball Grenades detonated and the car rollers howled as the rubber balls pummeled them.

Unda kept the truck crawling forward, while Bolan and Blancanales rolled along in outrider positions. Rocks and bottles and eggs pelted the Suburban as people found the moving vehicle in their midst and focused on it as a target for their rage. But when the crowd got too thick, the windows cracked once again and the sting-ball munitions dropped. People, ran, shouted, swore slogans, broke windows and set things alight, though the majority milled like sheep crazed by the sun and the shepherd and his dog had taken the day off.

Among the swarming sheep, Bolan and Blancanales scanned for the wolves. Suddenly Blancanales rasped over the radio, "Striker! On the convoy's three! Coming right at you!"

Bolan turned to see a pair of men rushing forward, wearing sunglasses and bandannas pulled up over their faces like bandits. Each man held low along his leg what looked to be a malt liquor tall can on a stick. In the smoke and gas they could easily be mistaken for bottles except the contraptions were painted Russian-military brownish-green. Bolan instantly recognized them as Russian RKG-3 antitank grenades. The Russian grenade would fry a Suburban and everyone inside. The lead grenadier hunched over his weapon and pulled the pin as he got within throwing distance.

Bolan shoved his BXP submachine gun out at arm's length and fired.

The man staggered as the burst walked up his side. The crowd's screaming turned to hysteria when the grenade went off and sheared away the man's head and shoulders.

The second grenadier was left staring in stunned horror at his comrade's partial incineration. He just managed to turn as Bolan gunned his bike forward and burned a burst from the BXP into the man's chest and dropped him to the street. He rolled up to the dead man and took the man's fallen grenade.

Bolan heard two quick bursts from Blancanales's weapon and saw a second pair of grenadiers drop to the pavement on the far side of the street. "Fire in the hole!" Blancanales shouted.

Smoke and fire blasted from the pulled grenade, but luckily people were already running away from the scene and straight into the police line, away from the convoy. Suddenly the street directly before them became a ghostly wasteland of black smoke, gray gas, smashed-in shops and burning, overturned vehicles.

The wolves loped through the carnage.

Bolan shouted across the secure channel. "Hostiles! Dead ahead!"

Men spilled out of the alleys girding both sides of the street ahead. They wore bandannas and sunglasses and carried M-16 rifles. They sprayed their weapons in long bursts as they came, and bullets chewed into Suburban's grille. They had spotted Blancanales and tracers streaked through the smoky murk toward him. Blancanales tipped over his Harley and took cover. Sparks whined off the chrome as he returned fire over the hog's massive engine block. Bolan then leaped from his own bike and knelt with one shoulder leaned against the marginal cover of a lamp-post. He brought his weapon to his shoulder and cut down two gunmen. Rifles swiveled in his direction.

The tail car of the convoy swerved around the Suburban and roared forward with tires screaming. The cops escorting them might be dirty, but in the maelstrom of the fight and their own people under fire they had rediscovered their duty and honor. The passenger window was open and the cop riding shotgun was firing his service pistol as fast as he could pull the trigger. Bolan burned down another rifleman and ejected his spent magazine. His eyes flared wide as he reloaded and he roared across the open channel, "Back! Back! Back!"

The Impala's tires shrieked in protest as the driver stood on the breaks and screamed again as he threw the car into Reverse and put the gas pedal to the floor. A man had popped up from behind a parked car and raised a weapon in his hands.

Olive drab cylinders like scuba tanks were strapped to his back.

The cop in the car fired his pistol dry and desperately slithered back inside the car as a long plume of flame whooshed from the flamethrower's projector. The Impala screamed backward as a twenty-foot-tall inferno burned across its hood. Bolan slammed in a fresh magazine and rose from his slender cover and yanked a rifle grenade out of his saddlebag.

There was no place to hide from a flamethrower. The only recourse was to run away out of range or to go forward and kill the man wielding it.

Bolan charged.

"All units! Covering fire! Load frag and forward!"

Unda, Constante and Gustolallo spilled out of the Suburban with weapons firing. The doors of the Impala flew open, and the two cops fell out of the burning vehicle coughing and covering their faces. They rolled away from the inferno and to their credit rose with the pistols in their hands.

Bolan fired his frag grenade at the VW Bug the flame-thrower guy crouched behind, and the little car rocked as the exploding grenade slammed shrapnel against it. Bolan charged with his weapon, spraying short bursts. Blanca-nales was right behind him, ignoring the hornet swarm of bullets whizzing around him. He kept his eye firmly on the Bug and the guy with the flamethrower behind it.

The man suddenly rose and Blancanales fired, but the problem with a rifle grenade was that you could actually see it spiraling toward you. So the flamethrower man shouted and dropped back down as the grenade slammed into his cover.

Neither Constante nor any of his crew had any protection against the gas and smoke but through streaming eyes they poured lead at any muzzle flash they saw. Bolan and Blancanales advanced implacably and some of the gunmen threw down their rifles, broke cover and ran.

Bolan noted with interest that one of them was well over six feet tall and his long black hair flew behind him as he ran. It seemed that Yotuel d'Nico had taken a personal interest in the day's events and had now suddenly lost interest. Bolan noted his direction of flight but kept running toward the flamethrower.

"Juice! Bring my bike!"

Blancanales began unloading his BXP into the BMW on full-auto. Bolan closed the distance. He vaulted onto the hood and stepped onto the roof. The flamethrower man lifted his bandanna-wrapped head and Bolan blew it off. The rest of the riflemen broke and ran.

With a grunt Bolan heaved one of the flamethrower straps over his shoulder. Gustolallo appeared by his side, limping and rolling his bike to him. She coughed and wept from the gas and smoke. "What are you—"

"Thanks." Bolan threw a leg over the bike and kicked the engine into life. He peeled away down the alley into which the Lion had disappeared. Amid the lines of drying laundry and heaps of garbage, Bolan glimpsed Yotuel's running figure. The Lion had ripped away his bandanna and he looked back over his shoulder with streaming eyes and a grimacing face as he ran and coughed. He had thrown away his rifle, but he drew a pistol and fired several wild shots at his pursuer.

Bolan reached into his saddlebag and drew the antitank grenade he'd confiscated. Yotuel shot another glance backward just as Bolan raised the grenade overhead. The soldier swung the two-pound stick grenade like a medieval mace and slammed him between the shoulder blades in passing. Yotuel was hurled facefirst into a cluster of garbage cans. Bolan spun the motorcycle into a screaming 180-degree halt. The Executioner put back the grenade, flicked down the kickstand and dismounted. Bolan took off his helmet. "Lion? You're going to talk to me."

Yotuel rose groggily from amid the garbage. He had lost his pistol, but he drew the conquistador lance head from beneath his belt, pointing the two feet of ancient iron at Bolan defiantly. "You think you scare me, white boy? You think you and all your Yanqui friends can—"

His voice trailed off as Bolan took the flamethrower's projector unit in both hands and raised it to his shoulder. Yotuel's pupils contracted to pinpricks of terror as he recognized the weapon, and the antique shank fell from his hand. "No, no man. Don't do it, don't…"

Bolan's voice was as cold as the grave. "You know the old saying about people who play with fire?"

The Lion raised palsied hands in supplication. "No! Jesus! *Madre de Dios,* no!"

Bolan squeezed the flamethrower's trigger. "They get burned."

Yotuel d'Nico staggered as the high-pressure jet of gasoline and diesel oil hit him like a fire hose and shoved him back against the wall of the alley. His feet flew from underneath him and he sat back down, drenched with jellied fuel. Bolan took his finger off the trigger. Yotuel had already taken lungfuls of tear gas and smoke and now he vomited as concentrated gasoline filled his nose and mouth. He twitched and clawed at himself as the clinging diesel oil stopped the gasoline from evaporating and kept it burning and tingling against his skin like a hellish rash.

Bolan waited.

There was very little that was lionlike about Yotuel d'Nico as he finally gasped and looked up from hands and knees. Bolan sighted down the flame projector, squeezed the igniter and the flamethrower's electrical ignition snapped like a gas stove about to light, then his finger curled around the projector's fuel trigger.

"I'm going to count to three."

13

"Move!"

Bolan dragged the Lion out of the alley with one fist in his mane and the antique edge at his back. He marched Yotuel to a parked cab, flung open the door and tossed the flamethrower in the back seat and his saddlebags to the floor.

The driver's head nearly hit the roof as he jumped in his seat. *"Madre de Dios!"*

Bolan snarled at the cabbie as he shoved the Lion into the back. "Drive!"

Bolan gave him the address Yotuel had spilled. The driver glanced back fearfully in his rearview once and then twice at his fare. The third time his eyes pierced the face distorted with swelling and covered with black oil, the cabbie's eyes went wide. The mighty figure of *El León* was well-known on the streets of San Juan. The cabbie threw a fearful glance at Bolan and shuddered as he took in eyes as blue as Antarctic ice with the whites eclipsed by bloody red veins. Bolan mercifully tilted his head toward the street. "Go."

But the man stopped at the next light and exploded out the door of his cab and didn't stop running. Bolan took a fistful of Yotuel's hair and hauled him out of the cab and deposited him behind the wheel. "You drive." The soldier slid back into the passenger seat and placed the lance blade at the nape of his prisoner's neck. "And if you betray me, *chico,* I'm going to light a match."

Yotuel hawked, spit blood into the passenger seat beside him and weakly shoved the cab into gear. Bolan spoke into his tactical radio to Blancanales. "You have me?"

"Affirmative, I have you on GPS tracker working a hundred percent. My bike got shot up pretty bad. I left it and am tailing you on yours."

"Roger that. I'm in a yellow cab heading east." Bolan responded. "Unda, you read?"

"I read you, Cooper."

"Get moving and stay on original course. The enemy will have informants on the street, and I want them to see you deliver Constante to the CIA San Juan Station as planned. I want them to think they know what we're up to for as long as possible."

"Affirmative, Cooper. We're moving. ETA CIA station ten minutes."

Blancanales spoke again. "I have a visual on you, Striker. I'm about seventy-five yards back."

Bolan looked back and saw him on the motorcycle about a block back. Bolan turned his attention back to Yotuel. "You got a phone number?"

"What?" He blinked and rubbed at his inflamed eyes. "I—"

"You're going to call in," Bolan instructed him. "You're going to say you made it out and need sanctuary. You're going to tell them you're holed up at your place."

Yotuel's eyes teared and blinked as he scowled. "My place?"

"The one up in the hills," Bolan said. "You know, the one where your little brother ran to meet you at after I kicked his ass."

Yotuel's shoulders hunched as the import of that hit him. "Listen, *señor,* we can—"

Bolan pressed the lance against the last vertebrae between the Lion's spine and his skull. "Make the call, then shut up and drive."

The Lion did as he was told. Yotuel d'Nico had a well-earned reputation for savagery and toughness but at the moment Bolan had him intimidated. Once up the mountain, the Lion parked outside his lair. He started to say something, but Bolan interrupted. "Who's home?"

"What? No one. I—"

"No one? No one at all?" Bolan kept the blade on the Lion's neck and raised the BXP in his other hand so the criminal could see it.

The Lion spoke through clenched teeth. "No one. I sent the servants back to their *barrios* for the weekend."

"Good." Bolan withdrew the blade, thrust it beneath his belt and shouldered the flamethrower. "Out."

Bolan followed the man up his drive and into his mansion "So—"

"So show me the money."

"What mon—" He buckled as Bolan's fist crashed into his kidney.

Bolan unslung the flamethrower and threw down his saddlebags. "Show me the money," Bolan said.

The Lion rose painfully and Bolan followed him to the master bedroom. D'Nico opened his closet and pushed aside some suits to reveal a small control panel. He punched numbers, and the back wall of the walk-in closet slid aside to reveal a very well-appointed safe room. One wall had an open foldout table with a phone and a laptop. An arsenal of rifles, pistols and shotguns were racked on the far wall, and a shelf below them contained pyramids of loaded magazines and boxes of ammunition. The third wall of the room was made up of shelves loaded with banded stacks of one-hundred-dollar bills. Bolan shoved Yotuel into the lone chair in front of the desk and picked up a stack of bills at random. He peeled off the top note and looked at it carefully while the Lion glowered from his seat.

The bill was one of the 1990-1995 design series, but it looked a little too virginal for currency that had been in circulation for thirteen to eighteen years. Bolan gave Benjamin Franklin a long hard look and then eyed the serial numbers.

Yotuel's reddened eyes widened in alarm as he realized what Bolan was doing. "What the…?"

Bolan smiled sadly as he examined the Federal Reserve and Treasury Seals and found what he had suspected. On the Treasury Seal the bottom three sawteeth that ran like sun rays around it were blunt rather than crisp and sharp like the rest. "Did you know the revolution is being funded with counterfeit money?"

"What the…?"

Bolan tossed the stack of hundreds back onto the shelf. "That's Iranian. Last I heard they were laundering it in Europe through the Turkish syndicates and in the Americas through the Colombians."

"What the…?" Yotuel repeated.

"Of course, the Colombian cartels have suffered a lot of setbacks in the past year. It's not surprising the Iranians have switched to funneling their counterfeit through Venezuela." Bolan waggled his eyebrows at the gangster. "No surprise at all the *venezolanos* would pay a piece of crap like you with toilet paper. Hell, they're going to turn you all into their peons anyway. This isn't a revolution, Yotuel, this is a hostile takeover. You've been played."

The Lion finally managed to complete a sentence. "What the fuck?"

"What?" Bolan shrugged. "You didn't know?"

It was very clear the crime lord didn't.

"Listen up." Bolan inclined his head toward the door. "Your friends are coming. Most likely they're coming to kill you because you and your little brother have been nothing but liabilities for the past few days." Bolan paused. "Say, where is your little brother anyway?"

Yotuel's jaw clamped shut.

"Okay." Bolan spoke into his tactical radio to Blancanales. "Hey, where's Yotuel's little brother?"

There was a pause as Yotuel glowered, and outside Blancanales checked his GPS tracker. "GPS has him…" An amused note passed through Blancanales's voice. "Has him coming up the mountain, actually."

Bolan looked at the Lion. "He's on his way. With your buddies. I wonder why?"

Yotuel's face darkened as he figured it out. "The little shit would not dare."

"Well, you know little Nacho." Bolan shook his head. "He's a weak suck, with a weak mind. Plus he's got a broken arm and is currently operating on cocaine, alcohol and painkillers. Oh, and you know something else? He's tired of being the weak suck in your shadow. I guarantee you he's looking for a way out of his current predicament, and I'm thinking the *venezolanos* may have made him an offer he can't refuse." Bolan waved his BXP questioningly. "But I don't know. What do you think?"

It was very clear what Yotuel "the Lion" d'Nico was thinking. His face was slowly purpling with rage beneath the bruises and black swaths of diesel oil.

Blancanales spoke in Bolan's earpiece. "I have vehicles on the road. Convoy of three. SUVs, tinted windows. How do you want to play it?"

Bolan considered. "How many of those RKG-3s did you pick up?"

He sounded pleased. "I have three."

Three was the magic number. "You got time to throw your saddlebags over the fence?"

"I'm on it."

Bolan nodded to Yotuel. "Get up."

The man started to rise and folded, dry-heaving, to the floor, wheezing in weak protest as Bolan hog-tied him with plastic restraints. The soldier took Yotuel's phone and plugged a Bluetooth transmitter into the interface. He set it by Yotuel's head. "I'll bet anything your brother's going to call in a minute. I'm going to leave you here with the door open. If you want to live, tell him you're in the kitchen. If he tells you to come out, you tell him to come in. You do that much without screwing up, and I'm going to let you live. Got it?"

"How the fuck am I supposed to answer it?" the gangster shouted.

"You can press the button with your tongue, your nose or whatever comes naturally. I don't care. Just remember I'll be listening, and I have a flamethrower."

Bolan rose and went downstairs. He picked up his saddlebags and the flamethrower and continued outside. Blancanales's bag came sailing over the wall on cue.

"Package received," Bolan said. He pulled his gear into a pile and crouched by the adobe wall near the gate.

Blancanales spoke a moment later. "I'm back in position. Enemy convoy on the road and continuing approach. ETA twenty seconds."

"Copy that." Bolan collected antitank grenades and waited. He heard the rumble of V-8 HEMI engines, then they all stopped simultaneously. Blancanales spoke very quietly in Bolan's ear. "All three vehicles have stopped short of the gate."

Bolan could hear Yotuel's phone ringing in his earpiece. When Yotuel finally answered, he snarled in Spanish and there was nothing fake about the anger in his voice. "What!"

Nacho spoke across the line. "Hey, brother. You okay?"

"No, everything went to hell! The Yanquis got Constante through! We have to get out of here. Maybe go chill out in Mexico."

So far Yotuel was playing his role. Nacho's voice was too sly for his own good. "Where are you, Yotuel? In the safe room?"

"No," the elder brother replied. "I'm in the kitchen. Why?"

"Nothing, I have a car. I'll be there in fifteen minutes."

Blancanales spoke across the private channel. "The sun roofs on the SUVs are opening. Striker, be advised, you have an RPG-7 gunner rising out of each vehicle."

"Copy that." Bolan looked up as launching charges thudded just behind the wall. The rocket-propelled grenades jumped through the air, and the three antitank rockets sizzled across the front lawn, crashing through the kitchen bay window that faced the driveway. The air shook as fire and smoke blasted outward from the front and side windows of the kitchen. Bolan crooked the three antitank grenades between the fingers and thumb of his left hand and vaulted up into a saddle position on the eight-foot adobe wall. Two shiny silver Lincoln Navigators and an Aviator were parked perpendicular to the wall with their bumpers almost touching it. Three grinning men wearing sunglasses stood up in the sunroofs with spent and smoking RPG-7 launch tubes across their shoulders. The grins fell from their faces and their jaws dropped open as they contemplated the red-eyed, grenade-laden apparition that had materialized on top of the wall before them.

The rocketeers dropped their launchers as Bolan began pulling pins.

Two of them slithered back into their vehicles and the man in the middle clawed for the pistol under his belt. Bolan lazily lobbed the grenades one-two-three from hood to hood. The bombs detonated one after the other like a three-stick string of dynamite. Bolan took up his BXP. "Pol, sitrep."

"All three vehicles burning, Striker. No, wait..." Amusement came into his voice once more. "You know? That boy is as hard to kill as a cockroach."

Bolan stood up and went out the gate.

Nacho d'Nico had fallen out the back window of the Aviator. His broken arm was still in a sling and in his other hand he was white-knuckling a revolver. The young man lunged to his feet like a motivated drunk and began to half run, half stumble down the mountain road.

Blancanales rose out of the underbrush and Nacho screamed liked an animal as the Able Team commando clotheslined the younger d'Nico across his already broken arm. Nacho's screaming was cut short as his skull bounced off the asphalt. Bolan quickly scanned each vehicle. The trucks were burned-out hulks and their passengers were charred husks. Nacho d'Nico had been thrown into the back cargo compartment of the Aviator like the garbage he was and that had saved his life.

Blancanales scooped up the dazed young criminal and threw him over one shoulder like a sack of potatoes. "What now?"

Bolan looked back at the Casa d'Nico. Fire was licking up the sides of the house from both smashed-out kitchen windows. They needed to get Yotuel out fast.

14

CIA Safehouse

Bolan stood staring at his captives, Yotuel's ancient wedge of iron at his side. The level of Spanish obscenities had risen to a crescendo. In the family room, the d'Nico brothers were tied to chairs facing each other with just enough space between them so they couldn't tip over their seats and start biting each other. The Lion was roaring like his nickname. Nacho's shrieking had risen to teakettle levels.

Bolan figured they were nicely primed and called out to the back of the house, "Let's bring in the next guest of honor!" A moment later Roldan and Unda escorted in the shooter Bolan had concussed with the butt of his BXP at the ranch-house fight. Nacho stared stupidly in nonrecognition. The shooter's raccoon-bruised eyes flared as he saw Yotuel. Bolan was almost afraid the Lion would burst his restraints as he roared and tried to rise up out of the chair he was tied to.

They'd had contact, all right.

A stream of invectives flew from Yotuel's mouth. The shooter stared long and hard at the Lion and kept his mouth clamped shut just as he had when they'd tried to interrogate him at the hospital. Bolan kept his eye on the shooter's face and let Yotuel's tirade grow in viciousness and volume and waited for the Lion to inadvertently press the magic button.

The man went involuntarily rigid when Yotuel called him "Venezuelan scum."

Bolan smiled.

The Lion saw the reaction as well and ran with it. He shouted at wall-shaking, patriotic decibels that Puerto Rico would never fall into the hands of the Communist whores in Caracas, and that he, Yotuel, was a Taino and a Boricua and the man before him was nothing but Venezuelan assassin scum.

The meet and greet had gone exactly as Bolan had hoped. The Lion had roared out things he wasn't supposed to know about. Bolan knew a great deal about reading body language, and a number of his suspicions had been confirmed by the shooter's reactions. People in Caracas were definitely involved, and the shooter from the ranch house was indeed Venezuelan assassin scum.

"Roldan, Unda, keep an eye on these guys." Bolan inclined his head toward the back porch, and he and Blancanales walked out into the night and looked at the lights of San Juan. Bolan turned to Blancanales. "So what do you think?"

"Oh, he's Venezuelan, all right. Except a flinch, a facial tic and a heartbeat of freeze up aren't exactly the kind of proof the President or the Joint Chiefs are going to accept."

"I know," Bolan agreed. "And?"

"And he's tough. He isn't talking."

Bolan agreed with all of that, but he looked slyly at Blancanales. "So you're buying my Venezuelan conspiracy theory now, aren't you?"

Blancanales leaned over the railing and took in the night air. "Funny you should mention that. Our friend inside isn't talking, but Canelo, the guy who was with Mustache? There was something strange about him."

"Like what?"

"His accent, for one."

"It was Venezuelan?"

"No." Blancanales shook his head. "He didn't sound Venezuelan, so I filed away what he said and how he said it to try to identify it later. I've been chewing over that conversation for hours."

Bolan knew Blancanales was on to something. "And what did you come up with?"

"This is going to sound weird, but what was strange wasn't his accent, but his lack of one," Blancanales continued. "His speech was a cipher, like a linguistic ghost, if you will. It was odd. I was almost ready to chalk it up as a random speech anomaly, but then I remembered that neither Nacho nor any other scumbag we've run into could identify the mystery men they've been meeting, and our scumbags deal with criminals from all over South America. When I read your report, it got me thinking. You've been talking about a Venezuelan conspiracy for the past forty-eight hours. Now I know the Venezuelans have been saying a lot of crazy things for the past couple of years, but despite their rhetoric and saber rattling, the U.S. still buys nearly three-quarters of Venezuela's crude-oil production. At the end of the day everyone knows whose dollars are buttering their bread." Blancanales made a fifty-fifty gesture with his hand. "At the same time the Venezuelans are doing some things that bear some real scrutiny. One of which is reorganizing their special forces, and they've been doing it with a lot of help from People's Republic of China."

Bolan saw where this was going. "Yeah, and?"

"And one thing the Chinese have always emphasized is their infiltration units. They've worked very hard for decades to come up with dedicated commando groups that can pass for locals." Blancanales sighed. "The Chinese

have long believed in being able to send in dedicated, po-
litically loyal troops who can pass for locals to carry out
sensitive missions."

Bolan had been on the wrong end of Chinese infiltration troops more times than he cared to remember. "So you
think Caracas is working up infiltration teams on the
Chinese model."

"They've openly stated they intend to spread the New
Bolivarian Revolution across South America and the Caribbean. Now it takes time to work up infiltration units that
can walk and talk like locals. But quick and dirty? You
could send your commandos to language school to eliminate their most obvious native-born mannerisms and into-
nations. In this case, sort of an accent-neutral Spanish
'battle language' for their commandos to use in foreign
countries. Of course, at best it would be a one- or two-trick
pony before the inflection-neutral battle language itself
was clearly identifiable by CIA linguists, but—"

"But ripping Puerto Rico right off its moorings and
turning it into a socialist satellite state dependent on Venezuelan oil money to stay afloat would be one hell of a one-
trick wonder," Bolan finished.

"Yeah, anyway, that's my own personal Venezuelan conspiracy theory." Blancanales spread his hands. "You like it?"

"Actually, I think we should run this by Bear," Bolan
replied.

"Me, too."

15

The d'Nico brothers had settled down to sullen glares and occasional, hoarsely whispered threats and imprecations. The Venezuelan commando sat mute, ignoring the d'Nicos and burning a hole through the wall with his eyes.

Bolan and Blancanales were huddled discussing the conversation Bolan had just had with Kurtzman. They'd come up with a theory on how the Venezualans were inserting their men. Blancanales rose without a word and walked up silently behind the Venezuelan. "So where are you guys landing your subs?"

Every muscle in the commando's body locked.

Blancanales continued conversationally, "I might be tempted to start off on the island of Vieques. It's sparsely populated, just a ten-mile hop to the main island, and ever since the U.S. Navy ceased using it for a bombing range most of it is wildlife refuge. Hell, there are stretches where unexploded U.S. ordnance means not even the park rangers visit. Is that where you and your buddies hang out and recover from your minisub ride across the Caribbean?"

Bolan folded his arms across his chest. "Nice."

The Venezuelan wouldn't meet Blancanales's eyes, but he smoldered in his seat with palpable hatred.

"Tell me, how many men you got out on Vieques? A squad? Platoon strength?"

The man on the chair exploded with rage. "You cannot

stop the revolution! What Simón Bolívar started and the capitalist multinationals corrupted we will finish and make clean!" The commando shook with emotion. He turned eyes burning with fanatical fervor on Bolan. "As for your precious United States? The *Reconquista* has already begun!" The Venezuelan commando looked at Bolan as if he were holding victory in his own handcuffed hands. "You are all dead men."

Bolan turned to Blancanales and saw concern in the warrior's eyes.

Roldan looked back and forth between the two men. "What?"

Bolan grabbed a heavy, black gear bag off the floor and heaved it onto the kitchen table. "We're about to get hit."

Unda's hand went to his Glock as he looked around in sudden concern and confusion. "Hit? How?"

Bolan shook his head as he unzipped his bag and began pulling out ordnance. "They tracked us. You two had better gear up. I don't think we have much time."

Roldan shared Unda's disbelief. "How? We searched him. He had nothing on him. You had the doctor give him a full-body MRI. If he had a tracker implanted in him, it would have lit up like Christmas."

"That's right." Blancanales grabbed his own bag and began rummaging. "They didn't track the Venezuelan."

Bolan slapped a magazine into his rifle and racked the action on a live round. "The Venezuelans put a tracer on Constante. We should have figured they could put one on Nacho. Hell, we did."

Nacho blinked uncomprehendingly. "What?"

Yotuel d'Nico was learning there was no bottom to the depths his little brother could disappoint him. There was no anger left in him. He just shook his head bitterly. "Brother, you have killed us."

Bolan powered up his rifle's optics. "Nacho, did they give you anything?"

"Who…gave me what?" Nacho stammered.

"When you agreed to help kill your brother, did the men you were with give you anything? Cigarettes? A gun? Anything?"

"No, I had my own, no, wait. I needed a light." Nacho sat up straight. "A lighter! I needed a light and the man who gave it to me told me to keep it!"

Bolan went to the kitchen counter. There were two plastic salad bowls filled with the things they had taken from Yotuel and Nacho. Bolan took a lighter out of the bowl of Nacho's effects. It was a cheap, plastic disposable job with a topless woman on it. Bolan dropped the lighter to the kitchen floor and crushed it under his boot.

He looked long and hard at Yotuel. "Hey, Lion."

Yotuel glared back sullenly. "What?"

"All that about you being Boricuas, Taino and Puerto Rico forever? You mean it?"

An angry retort almost came out of the Lion's mouth. He bit it back as he suddenly intuited what Bolan was asking. "Yeah, I mean it. Puerto Rico forever." He glared at the Venezuelan. "And payback."

Even Blancanales was appalled. "You gotta be kidding."

"We're about to get hit. They know I'm here. They know the Lion's here." Bolan glanced at the Venezuelan. The shooter was smiling. "They know he's here, and now they know that we know. They're going to hit us with everything they've got. Constante and Gustolallo aren't here and I need every Puerto Rican patriot." Bolan shook his head at Nacho. "Except him."

"Hey!"

Bolan ignored the younger d'Nico. "So tell me, Yotuel. You in?"

The Lion nodded. "I'm in."

Roldan made a face but kept silent as Bolan picked up the ancient lance blade and sliced through Yotuel's restraints. He stabbed the blade into the arm of the Lion's chair while d'Nico rubbed his wrists. Looking at Blancanales, Bolan said, "Give him a gun."

"I saw you shooting an M-16 during the riot." Blancanales pulled out a Heckler & Koch 416. "This isn't much different." The Lion thrust his blade under his belt and took the weapon. He racked the action with practiced ease.

"And a pistol."

Blancanales took out one of the .45s they'd confiscated. The Lion rose to his full height, armed with rifle, pistol and blade. "We kill them. We kill them all."

Roldan shrugged into his blue SWAT-issue armor. "So what's the plan?"

"The Venezuelans are coming. We have a valuable prisoner," Bolan said. "They don't get him back. This is a siege. We repel all boarders."

Unda cocked his Uzi and began shoving spare magazines into his pockets and under his belt. "Where do you want us?"

Bolan considered their castle and its defenses. It was up in the hills, and you could look in on the hillside mansions of a number of Puerto Rican politicos and drug dealers and penthouses in the city below with high-powered optics. The house hung from the hillside with much of it supported by twenty-foot, cross-braced steel stilts. It would be very hard for the enemy to get behind them. But the stilts allowed the possibility of the enemy getting underneath. He wished Constante and Gustolallo were here. He really wished he had Flaco Ordones and his Browning machine rifle backing them up. He looked over his local allies. "You Boricuas take the front approach. Keep your eyes on the road and keep me informed. I'm going to go see what's going on down the hill a little."

Bolan took a coil of rope from one of his bags and tied it fast to the barbecue pit sunk into the patio deck. He stepped to the porch rail and hurled the coil to the steeply sloping hillside twenty feet below. The supersonic crack of a rifle bullet passed inches from his ear. Bolan dropped low and rolled back into the house.

"Unda, Roldan. Get out front. Keep the enemy off the house. Down is our best way out of here. I'll clear a path down the hill." He glanced at Yotuel. "Go with them. Do whatever they tell you."

The Lion scowled, but he followed the two cops out front. The second the door opened a hail of gunfire cut loose out on the road. Roldan's, Unda's and Yotuel's weapons all began firing.

Blancanales was reaching into his bag and pulled out his BXP. "Grenades?"

"Yeah." Bolan had brought along night-vision equipment. He figured the enemy would probably have it, too, but he doubted the Venezuelan commandos had brought along gas masks. Bolan had. "We drop tear gas and use frags on any muzzle flashes. Once the gas is spreading downhill I'll go over the side and start clearing a path. You cover me from up top. When I give you the signal, you get our Puerto Rican friends inside and gear them up with goggles and gas masks and get them down the rope fast. None of them have done any night-fighting, so you're pretty much going to have to shepherd them down the hill."

"Copy that."

"We're taking heavy fire out here!" Roldan yelled.

The shooters on the hillside suddenly seemed to be tired of waiting. Bullets ripped up at the house, chewing into the hanging porch.

"Rocket!" Unda roared. An RPG round slammed into the side of the safehouse. Stucco sifted down from the ceiling with the impact, but the the front of the house was adobe and there was hardly any better material for stopping a shaped charge weapon than a foot or two of clay. The bad guys wouldn't be able to burn down or blow up the house, but given enough time they might just pound the place to rubble.

Bolan and Blancanales clicked grenades onto their weapons and stepped out the sliding glass door to the hanging porch. They aimed their weapons high and arced the gas grenades to land close to the base of the house. They both reloaded and fired twice more. Blancanales frowned. "That's it for gas."

Bolan nodded as they stepped back. "Frag 'em." The two warriors stepped out onto the porch and fired once more. This time they aimed straight down the mountainside. The antipersonnel grenades cracked and flashed in the trees below. The wooden porch beneath their feet shivered as two more RPG rounds hit the front of the house.

"Yotuel, please!" Nacho screamed the same way a man dying on the battlefield might cry out for his mother. *"Hermano, por favor!"*

Bolan snatched a glance back as Yotuel burst back into the house. Bolan snapped another grenade onto his muzzle and snarled. "Get back on station!"

The Lion ignored him. Most of Yotuel's left ear had been shot away, and he was limping from a leg wound. He swore a blue streak as he drew his lance blade and slashed away Nacho's bonds. He yanked his little brother to his feet and shoved his .45 into Nacho's good hand. "Now you fight, *hermanito!*" the Lion roared. "We fight together! We fight like—"

Nacho shot his older brother in the head.

"Jesus!" Bolan raised his weapon, but the frag grenade was attached to it. "Pol!"

Blancanales whipped around but Nacho had fled. He shouted out toward the front. "Roldan, Unda! Nacho is AWOL and—"

Nacho's .45 barked seven times in rapid succession out on the front porch. Bolan shoved his grenade-laden weapon into Blancanales's hands. "Keep it up! I'll be back!" Bolan drew his machine pistol and loped to the front door. Nacho was running and screaming down the darkened mountain road. "Don't shoot! It's me! Nacho! I shot the Lion! I shot Unda! I shot Roldan!"

Bolan took his pistol in both hands and took aim as Nacho screamed and ran on. "The Yanqui and his friend are alone inside! Your man is alive and—"

Bolan needn't have bothered.

Nacho screamed as tracers streaked out of the trees and burned red laser lines into his body. He twisted and fell to the ground. Bolan fired a burst at one of the muzzle flashes strobing on the dark road and the weapon fell silent. Roldan and Unda were on their hands and knees behind the low porch wall groaning and clawing for their fallen weapons. The men had been shot in the back three and four times, respectively. They were wearing armor, but they'd taken the hits from behind and by surprise.

"In the house!" Bolan shouted. "Move! Move! Move!"

Bolan's battle command galvanized the two cops into action. They brought up their weapons and retreated through the front door while Bolan covered them and then hurled himself through the door. An RPG round sizzled after him in pursuit and missed flying through the open door by inches.

He had to get his team regrouped and break out down the mountain before the safehouse turned into the Alamo.

Blancanales's voice was the toll of doom. "Striker! We got a chopper approaching fast! He isn't broadcasting on the police band! He's—Jesus Christ!"

"Down!" Bolan boomed. The team dropped to the floor as bullets spewed from the air-mounted six-barreled weapon. Everything above waist height was instantly torn apart, including the Venezuelan commando's head. Railroad tracks of bullet craters stitched the walls faster than thought. The men out front were either making their approach or waiting for Bolan and his men to break out through the front door.

The Minigun barrels continued to spin and bullets tore through the house like a chain saw. Blancanales jerked his head toward the incoming fire. "The chopper is pinning us down!" He glanced to the front. "And the enemy is gonna storm us any second!"

Bolan agreed.

Blancanales nodded hopefully. "You've got an idea, right?"

Bolan did have an idea. Just not a very good one. "Yeah. That chopper has got to go!"

Blancanales stared at the obviousness of the statement. "You think?"

"Cover me!"

"Cover you?" Blancanales looked at his submachine gun and then risked a glance at the gunship outside spewing lead at six thousand rounds a minute. "Uh…okay!"

"No!" Bolan shouted. "Grenade!"

Blancanales shook his head. "We're out of antiarmor rounds! A frag can't crack that chopper, and we're going to come up short swapping lead with that Minigun!"

"No! Flare round! I just need you to freak him out enough to veer off for a few seconds so I can get to the porch!"

Blancanales scuttled for the grenade bag and clicked a flare round over the muzzle. He hunched down as a line of bullets ripped through the kitchen counter inches over his head. "Ready!"

Bolan holstered his Beretta and got into position like a sprinter at the starting blocks. "Now!"

Blancanales rose and fired. A red, incandescent ball of fire shot like a meteor through the house and out the shattered back window straight for the nose of the chopper. The pilot rammed his throttles full forward. He veered off and the flare round streaked past his fuselage. Bolan charged for the porch, snatching the flamethrower along the way. He seized the rope attached to the barbecue and flung himself out into space. It was a wild leap, and the rope burned like fire through his hand. The soldier dropped the twenty feet far faster than he'd wanted to, and he came up battered and reeling with no air in his lungs, but there was no time to assess the damage. He raised the flamethrower.

The helicopter orbited back in to continue its assault. It was an old Army Huey. The Minigun mounted on the starboard landing skid resumed the assault out front. The chopper was directly above him, and Bolan stood in the eye of the rotor-wash storm ready to fire. He squeezed the flamethrower's projector trigger.

Fire shot in a seventy-foot plume into the air and mushroomed against the belly of the chopper. The rotor vortex drew the jellied fuel inexorably up the sides of the helicopter and sucked it in through the open cabin doors. Jellied fuel was drawn up into the air intakes and coated the rotor blades, turning the helicopter into a windmill of fire with her engines screaming and choking on burning diesel oil and gasoline. Bolan held down the trigger until the fuel tanks were empty.

Shrugging off the spent flamethrower, Bolan moved back up the hill on leaden legs to get as far beneath the house as he could. A few bullets cracked past him, but the tear gas was spoiling the shooter's aim. The helicopter shuddered and tipped above as the pilot and copilot screamed and burned.

The flame-engulfed aircraft slewed into the porch.

The struts and braces groaned and flexed around Bolan. As flaming rotor blades snapped off and scythed down the mountain, the porch collapsed in a cascading bonfire. The burning airframe fell with it, and Bolan covered his face as the heat washed over him. The helicopter landed on its side and began rolling down the hillside, crushing several of the enemy shooters and leaving a trail of wet fire as it went.

"Striker!" Blancanales was shouting in Bolan's earpiece. "Striker!"

Bolan groaned. "Yeah."

"You okay?"

"Yeah, I'm in one piece."

Blancanales's voice was slightly awed. "You know, I think you're the first person in history to shoot down a helicopter with a flamethrower."

"We all have our strengths. On my signal get everyone shooting out front, like you're making a break for it. I'm going to get up behind them."

"Copy that."

Bolan drew his Beretta and clambered along the bottom of the house. He moved across the steep hillside just below the road. As he got some trees between himself and the fire down in the ravine, he pulled his night-vision goggles over his eyes. Bolan limped and stumbled a hundred yards along the hillside and then made his way up onto the road and across it to the shelter of the trees on the other side. He could see eight men moving in all along the frontage of the house. Scanning the hillside, Bolan found the machine gun not far from his position. The gunner's attention was totally absorbed by the house. Bolan whispered into his mike, "Start shooting."

The bullet-riddled front door flew open and Unda's Uzi rattled off a long burst.

Every enemy weapon opened up.

Bolan trudged up the hillside. The machine gunner was behind an M-60. He snatched off short bursts through the front door and the front windows with well-practiced aplomb. He also sensed Bolan behind him, but his weapon was far to heavy to lift and turn in time. Bolan punched a three-round burst between the man's shoulder blades, and he fell back across his weapon. Bolan pushed the gunner over with his boot and closed his hand around the M-60's carrying handle.

Bolan began moving down the hill in a diagonal line toward the house. He walked up to a man aiming an RPG and shot him in the back of the head. The second RPG man flinched at the sound of a pistol behind him and turned. Bolan gave him a burst through the throat and moved on for the men on the road. "Pol, RPGs are down. Hillside is clear. You got gunners on the road. Hit them when you hear an M-60."

"Copy that," Blancanales came back.

Bolan holstered the Beretta, dropped to one knee and brought the M-60 to bear. He began pumping bursts into the gunmen on the road. The gunmen turned as the machine gun began burning through their ranks. Blancanales, Unda and Roldan came out the front door firing. Bolan was somewhat surprised to see Yotuel reeling after them like a hamburger-faced zombie out of a horror movie. The men on the road were caught in the cross fire. Within six seconds the gunners were either moaning or dead on the mountain road. It took all of Bolan's strength to stand back up with the M-60 in his hands, but the weight of the weapon was more than he could bear so he dropped the machine gun and drew his Beretta.

Blancanales walked up to him and gave him a long look that was half awe and half concern. "You all right?"

"Yeah, just a little weary," Bolan conceded.

Blancanales glanced at the commandos littering the road. "Well, one of these guys might make it. I'm calling in medevac."

Bolan glanced at Yotuel d'Nico. The Lion looked like a man who was standing against a strong wind. His brother's bullet had chipped the corner of his left eye and apparently burrowed along the side of his skull and took what remained of his ear with it.

"You should sit down," Blancanales suggested.

Bolan had to admit it wasn't a bad idea.

16

Guistina Gustolallo slipped into Bolan's hotel room, stripped off her clothes and joined him on the bed. "Sorry I missed the fun."

"I could have used you and that shotgun of yours," Bolan admitted.

"And how is your hand?" She picked up Bolan's bandaged left hand.

"Oh, it'll be fine," Bolan said. "How's Yotuel?"

"He's in real bad shape. We're waiting to hear from the hospital," Gustolallo answered. "So, baby, what do you—" Gustolallo yelped as Bolan roughly shoved her away. The iron ax blade split the bed between them and sank through Tempurpedic foam. Bolan slapped his hand down across the ax shaft so the killer couldn't withdraw it and his left foot lashed up into the assassin's face. This *Orisha* wasn't wearing a ballistic motorcycle helmet, and his teeth flew from the impact. Bolan yanked on the ax but the *Orisha* heaved back with massive strength. Bolan resisted for just a moment, letting the killer pull him up and then suddenly let the weapon go. The man staggered back three steps and almost fell. It gave Bolan time to pull the Beretta 93-R from beneath his pillow.

The *Orishas* weren't just executioners. They were commandos, and someone had drilled them with their antique weapons. The cleaver hissed around and Bolan's hand went numb with the impact as ax met machine pistol. The

Beretta loosed a burst before spinning out of Bolan's grasp. The soldier leaned away from the back swing and gasped for breath. His lungs had been just about burned out of his body with chemicals, and he had been running and fighting for four days. He needed an edge and he needed it now.

Gustolallo jumped up on the bed like a gymnast hitting a pommel horse and sailed through the air in a flying tackle, but she was met midair by the razor-sharp black African iron. The detective made a terrible noise that was eclipsed in ugliness by the sound of the ax hitting her head. Gustolallo fell in a boneless tangle of limbs to the carpet. Bolan's insides went sick and cold, but he had no time for anything but the killer before him.

Bolan scooped Yotuel's conquistador blade from the dresser and got his feet on the floor.

The *Orisha* spoke, and he spoke in English for Bolan's benefit. "I'm going to cut off your head Yanqui, but first I'm going to cut off your *cojones*—"

Bolan threw. It wasn't a strong throw, but the lance head was six inches of empty socket with two feet of steel in front. It was supremely point heavy and flew like a lawn dart without revolving. The *Orisha* had been stupid enough to flap his gums, and Bolan made him pay for it. The point punched through the hollow of the *Orisha's* throat, sinking through the soft flesh and only stopping when the point met his spine. The assassin gagged and fell to his knees, reaching for the blade impaling his throat with shaking hands.

Bolan swatted aside the *Orisha's* palsied hands and ripped the blade free with a sideways yank. The assassin fell facefirst to the carpet.

The Executioner retrieved his fallen Beretta and crouched beside Gustolallo. There appeared to be no more attackers. Bolan knelt frozen in place with his machine pistol at the ready and felt a slight breeze across his face. A window was open. The enemy had come in through the balcony off the suite's main room. Bolan took his tactical flashlight off the bedstand and played it across Gustolallo's head. She was bleeding a river, but as he probed the wound with his fingers it was clear the ax had hit flat-edge on. She had still taken a pound and a half of iron upside the head, though, and there was no telling what had happened inside her skull. She let out a moan and he took that as a good sign.

Bolan found his phone and called Blancanales. He picked up on the first ring. "Yeah."

"Pol, Juice and I just got hit. *Orisha* style. She has a head injury and we need to medevac her someplace safe."

"On it," Blancanales said. And the line clicked off.

The detective moaned weakly. She brought a hand to her head and stared at the wet blood that instantly covered it. "What happened?"

"Some guy hit you in the head with an ax."

Gustolallo blinked and lost her English. *"Realmente?"*

"Yeah, really." Bolan took a pillowcase and pressed it to the side of her head.

Blancanales knocked three times. "It's me!"

Bolan covered Gustolallo with a sheet. "Clear!"

Blancanales came in with a locked and loaded BXP. "What's the situation?"

"Gustolallo has a concussion, and we've got a dead *Orisha* there on the carpet. I haven't swept the rest of the suite."

He nodded. "Stay with her." Blancanales swept the rest of the hotel suite. "Clear! The balcony window is open. You got a rope leading down to it from the roof. I'll sweep up top with Roldan and Unda."

"Hey."

Blancanales stopped in the foyer. "Yeah?"

"How did the *Orisha* know we were here?" Bolan's eyes went cold. "For that matter, how did they know which room I was in?"

"Unda!" Blancanales snarled. He didn't like dirty cops, much less triple-crossing ones.

Bolan nodded and punched a button on his phone. "Inspector, we've been hit. I need you, Unda and Roldan, my room, ASAP.

"We are on our away, amigo."

Bolan flicked on the light as feet thudded out in the hallway. The three Puerto Rican cops burst into the room and stopped at the sight of Detective Gustolallo lying on the floor covered with blood. Unda blinked in shock. *"Madre de Dios…"* Inspector Constante's face hardened into a cold mask of anger. Roldan was clearly horrified.

Bolan rose and pointed to the ax he tossed on the bed. "It was the *Orishas.*" Bolan suddenly knocked the Glock pistol out of Unda's hand and buried his stiffened fingers into the detective's guts like a spear. Unda wheezed as he took two faltering steps backward and his legs failed him.

Bolan aimed the Beretta between Unda's eyes. "We were betrayed, Unda."

The whites of the detective's eyes were very wide, but his brows were bunched in anger. "Fuck you. I didn't do shit." He lifted his chin at the muzzle of the Beretta bravely. "You gonna do me? You do it. But I tell you now, next time you sucker punch me I'll kill you."

Constante spit. "I should have done you days ago." He turned to Bolan. "I'll do it."

"No." Bolan kept his weapon leveled and turned to Roldan. "What do you say, Roldan? Should I do him?"

Roldan was still staring in shocked horror at Gusto-lallo. He snapped out of it and blinked. "Wh-what?"

"You didn't expect Gustolallo to be in my room, did you? You should be in a rage right now and be screaming bloody murder. Instead you look sick with guilt to me." Bolan pointed the machine pistol at Roldan like a judging finger. "What do they have on you that would make you turn traitor? I can't believe it would be money, or that you could be personally intimidated. What is it? Your family?"

Roldan buckled and fell to his knees. Tears of shame spilled down his cheeks. "They have my sister, Naida." Roldan's face fell into his hands and he just wept.

Unda was rubbing his wrist and glaring. "Can I get up now?"

"Yeah," Bolan said. "Sorry about that."

Unda collected his pistol and rose. "So what do we do?"

"Not much choice." Bolan holstered his pistol. "We get Roldan's sister back."

Roldan's head jerked up from his weeping. "We do?"

"The bad guys have got to be running low on *Orisha* as-sassins, and they've taken a lot of hits to their cadre of infil-tration troopers. Taking your sister was a simple snatch, but by the same token kidnapping a cop's sister is high profile. They wouldn't risk the exposure for such a small job."

Unda shrugged. "So who did it?"

Bolan looked long and hard at Unda. "Who do you think?"

Unda's shoulders sagged and he rolled his eyes. "Dirty cops."

"That's right. You want to blackmail a cop? Have other cops do the dirty work. Keep it in house and the code of silence prevails." Bolan returned his attention to Roldan. "Where did they grab her?"

"Our house."

"You have any witnesses?"

"*Sí*, Ola, our maid. She phoned me and gave me their message." Renewed shame shook him. "The message was just *'Give us the gringo'* and a phone number to call."

"Did the maid recognize them?"

"No, she just said two plainclothes policemen came to the door. I'd told her not to open the door for anyone, but they showed their badges and when she opened the door they came in, took Naida and gave her the message for me."

Bolan turned to Blancanales. "We need to get Ola in front of a sketch artist ASAP. Requisition one from the CIA or FBI." Bolan nodded at the Puerto Ricans. "As soon as we have the sketches, we've got to pray that one of you recognizes these guys and has an idea of where they might have taken Naida." Bolan looked down reluctantly at Gustolallo. "You up for it?"

"Uhh…" Gustolallo tried to push herself up and then laid back down again. "Sure."

Bolan made an ugly decision. "Inspector?"

"Yes?" Constante said.

"Bring Yotuel from the hospital."

Constante shook his head reluctantly. "He's not in good shape. He is in ICU and—"

"I don't care. If he's conscious, yank him."

17

Yotuel d'Nico looked like death warmed over. His pulped and burned-out eye was covered by an oozed-through bandage. The entire left side of his head was swollen, and stitches like railroad tracks covered the remaining shreds of his left ear. Unda, Roldan and Gustolallo had come up snake eyes on the sketches. Constante thought he might have seen one of the men depicted somewhere but he couldn't put a name to the face. It was understandable. Puerto Rico had the largest police department in the U.S. except for New York, with a myriad of divisions and offices.

The Lion was their last hope.

Bolan pushed the sketches before him.

Yotuel peered with bleary monocular vision at the police sketches. He hawked and spit blood on the floor. "Yes, I know those two. They were vice cops." The Lion turned one eye on Gustolallo. "Before her time. They were on the bunco squad. The bigger one, Hespero? Back in the day I used to pay him off."

"Hespero!" Constante placed the face. "I thought I knew him from somewhere! Years ago, he and I were in the same class testing for detective."

Yotuel stabbed a finger onto the second sketch. "The ugly one's name is Trujillo, but every calls him Feo."

"You said they used to be vice." Bolan gazed at the sketches. "What are they now?"

"Detectives with Internal Affairs." Yotuel's smile was grotesque. "If you are a dirty cop, what better job than to prey on other dirty cops?"

Blancanales scratched his chin. "So where would Hespero and Feo take Naida?"

Inspector Constante let out a long, tired breath. "Perhaps I know where she might be."

Bolan turned. "Oh?"

"*Sí.*" Constante nodded. "The Bastille."

Unda shifted uncomfortably. "*Madre de Dios,* Noah…"

Roldan stared with wonder. "I thought that was just a locker-room legend."

"Tell me about the Bastille," Bolan said.

"It is, indeed, almost a legend," Constante said. "They say there is an old Spanish fort up in the hills, little more than a ruin nicknamed the Bastille, and back in the day, it was a place where cops were sometimes taken. If you were not on the take, if you refused your take, and you made enough people nervous, you might be taken there, and your situation would be explained to you, very unpleasantly, by your fellow officers. They say the grounds around it are filled with the bodies of cops who could not be reasoned with." Constante lit a cigarette. "It was all a very long time ago, and all very old-school, almost a secret society in the department. I have not heard a rumor of an officer 'visiting' the Bastille in years and years. We live in different times now." The inspector blew smoke down upon the sketches. "But the Bastille is still the boogeyman, the dark place you might go to for not playing by the rules. Even the latest generation of Puerto Rican cops have heard whispers about the place. And men like Hespero and Feo are the kind who would know the place of old. They are the kind of men who would have been sent to fetch you there."

"Naida." Roldan was close to tears again at the thought of his sister in such a place and in the hands of such men. "Inspector, I beg you, where is the Bastille?"

"That is the problem." Constante shrugged unhappily. "I do not know. Once, as a young officer, I was put in a very uncomfortable position, and I chose a side. Two officers I did not know picked me up and told me I was wanted at headquarters, but it was soon very clear that was not where they were taking me. They took my gun and my knife, but they did not know about the razor I carry in my shoe. I cut one very badly before he knew what was happening and I jumped out of the car. To my shame, I turned my back on the situation, and later heard rumors the matter was considered closed. I believe the Bastille was my destination, but I am sorry, I do not know where to find it."

Roldan's fists shook with impotent rage. "Then how do we find it! How do wc find Naida!"

"We find a man." Bolan glacial blue eyes stared at the sketches. "A man like Hespero or Feo, and then we make him take us there."

Roldan surged to his feet. "I will go with you!"

Bolan shook his head. "No. No, you're all cops, and we're going to have to go all the way to the top to break open the Bastille. If it goes bad you're all dead, in jail or your careers ruined." Bolan sighed. "We got the *Orisha,* but there will be lookouts on the street. I need most of the team here to keep them busy. They know something has gone wrong, but they don't know what. There's a chance they'll wait and see, and that's the only chance your sister has. You stay here with the inspector, and be ready to move on my signal."

Constante frowned. "You're going to do this by yourself?"

"No, I'm taking my friend here and Yotuel. We need to find someone who would know where the Bastille would be. Inspector, give me the name of a man who would have to know about the Bastille, and I don't care how high up that name goes. Then we're going to pay him a visit."

Bolan looked over at Yotuel and handed him the conquistador blade. "I held on to this for you. You might need it."

JUDGE OLIVIER HONORE shot up in bed. His shout died in his throat as a pair of icy blue eyes fixed him place. The Yanqui looming at the foot of the bed held a huge pistol and looked toward the right side of the bed and spoke quietly. "Yotuel?"

The judge made a strangling noise as he looked up at the bloody, mutilated, long-haired cyclopean person standing over him with a two-foot spear blade.

"Sí?"

"Every time the judge says the word *no,* cut something off him."

"Sí."

The name Yotuel cut through the judge's sleep befuddled brain. The Lion was horribly wounded and in his bedroom. As for the Yanqui with the glacial gaze… *"Madre de Dios,"* the judge whispered.

Bolan held Honore's eyes like a cobra hypnotizing its prey. "The Bastille, Your Honor. You're going to take us there."

"What?" Honore shook his head. "What are you talking about?"

The judge jumped as Blancanales seemed to appear out of nowhere. "Amigo? You have fallen into the hands of unreasonable men. No, I take that back. You have fallen into the hands of determined men, and a young woman's life hangs in the balance. I suggest you choose your next words wisely."

Judge Honore paled. "What? I—" He shrieked as the lance point pressed just beneath his left eye socket.

Yotuel whispered in the judge's ear like a lover. "I lost my left eye tonight, and in 1989 you gave me a nickel in Río Piedras Prison. Now I—"

Bolan held up a restraining hand. "I said if he said *no.* Your Honor, I really want you to get this right. I want you to take us to the Bastille. Are you saying no?"

"Please say yes," Blancanales suggested. "It will work out so well for everyone."

The judge looked like a man drowning in quicksand. "I—"

Bolan cut him off and used the ammunition Constante had given him. "You were a bureau chief in the department before you became a jurist. That's quite a jump, and that was in the seventies. The good old days, before the cocaine trade took over everything. When a trip to the Bastille was just the ticket to set things straight and help a man get ahead."

"I don't know—" The judge shrieked again as Yotuel pressed the blade just beneath the Honore's left eye until blood came.

Bolan held up his hand again. "He said *know,* not *no.*"

The judge was close to gibbering. Bolan holstered his pistol. "Your Honor, if you say anything other than yes, my friend and I are going to walk away and leave you with *Señor* d'Nico." His voice dropped an ominous octave. "Will you, or will you not take us to the Bastille tonight?"

The Highlands

THE JUDGE'S MERCEDES 350SL cruised down dirt roads that had not seen any real traffic in quite some time. Honore's hands shook as he white-knuckled the wheel. The

Lion's lance pressed into his side might have had something to do with it. Bolan and Blancanales screwed foot-long suppressor tubes onto the business ends of their BXP submachine guns. "How many men?" Bolan asked.

"I…do not know."

"You've attended these functions before. How many men usually for a Bastille party?"

"That…would—" the judge spoke with difficulty "—depend."

Bolan pressed. "How about for an execution?"

"Few, the fewer the better. A couple of men the victim doesn't know to bring the man in off the street. A couple more as lookouts, maybe a helper or two if he was to suffer before he died."

Bolan's voice went cold. "And the rape and murder of a fellow officer's teenage sister?"

The judge fell silent. He yelped as Yotuel pressed the blade. "The man asked you a question."

The judge barely spoke above a whisper. "As many who wished to…participate."

Bile turned Bolan's voice as cold as the grave. "Fine, then. This is how we play it. It's a party and we're late. Judge, you and my friend are going to talk your way in the front door. Yotuel and I are going to sneak in."

"I see a light ahead," Blancanales said.

Bolan and Yotuel hunched in their seats. The soldier heard someone call out, and the Mercedes ground to a halt. Over the edge of the door Bolan could see the squat dark shape of a medieval tower looming up against the stars. The tower disappeared as a flashlight's glare hit the windshield and blotted out the night.

Blancanales and the judge slid out of the car and Honore called out. Bolan's stomach slowly turned as he listened to the conversation. Whoever the guard was, he was showing the judge deference. The judge was explaining that Blancanales was a very good friend and wanted to be a part of the proceedings. The good news according to the guard was that the fun had not started yet. Bolan pushed down cold rage.

The Executioner waited for a few seconds and his phone vibrated. He read the numeral 3 on the dimmed screen. It was Blancanales's signal. Bolan pulled on his night-vision goggles, opened the door and rolled out. The Bastille was a simple Spanish tower, part of which had collapsed inward, leaving it in the shape of a darkened, jagged tooth. Bolan scanned the area. Two men stood smoking cigarettes before the door. A third man was perched in the crumbling battlements above. All of them carried shotguns.

Bolan snapped out the BXP folding buttstock and brought the weapon to his shoulder. He peered up at the top of the tower and fired. The man on the battlements jerked as the 9 mm hollowpoint rounds hit him.

The men below jumped out of the way in shock as the topside lookout fell with a thud to the gravel before them.

Bolan rattled off two quick bursts and cut the other two guards down. Yotuel heaved himself out of the car with a groan and shambled over. The Executioner tossed him a shotgun. The Lion caught it awkwardly and put a hand on the crumbling stonework to steady himself. Bolan eyeballed his erstwhile enemy. "You ready for this?"

Yotuel was none too steady in his reply. "Yeah…but I feel sick."

Bolan held up one finger in the starlight. "How many fingers?"

The Lion took a few too many seconds to answer. "Two."

Double vision and nausea were very normal signs for a

man who had been shot in the head, but they didn't bode well for a combat operation. "Stay on my six, don't shoot unless I do. Got it?"

"*Sí*...I got your six."

Bolan moved. "Let's go." The inside of the tower was hollow with stone stairs spiraling up the inside to the battlement above. But the square hole in the floor leading down was of interest. Light flickered up out of it. A dungeon. Bolan pushed up his goggles and sped down the steep, wet stone steps. Harsh laughter rose from below and a woman screamed.

A gunshot echoed off the stone walls and Blancanales's voice roared, "Freeze!"

Several gunshots rang out. A woman screamed again. Blancanales's weapon went full-auto and a shotgun fired both barrels. Bolan hit the foot of the stairs and found himself in a narrow, dripping, stone-lined corridor lit with a string of shop lights. A partially open steel security door guarded the chamber end of the corridor. Inside he could hear men shouting. The judge was screaming that he'd been kidnapped. Someone shouted, "He's wearing armor" and a gun went off again.

Bolan kicked the door.

Blancanales sat against the wall. The front of his suit was shredded from the double shotgun blast. His weapon lay on the floor a few feet away, and a fat man was standing over him and pointing a Glock. Another man held the judge up by his lapels and shouted in his face. Of the six other men in the room one lay dead, four others milled about with pistols in their hands while the sixth spit on his fingers and plucked the smoking shells from a sawed-off double-barrel 10-gauge. A young woman with a riot of copper curls and copper skin like Roldan's hung by her hands from chains in the ceiling like something out of the Spanish Inquisition.

Bolan swung his sights onto the man holding iron on Blancanales and put a five-round burst through the side of his head.

Blancanales flinched as the fat man's head was hammered apart. He reached up and ripped the weapon from the dead man's hand, as the obese officer fell on top of him. Bolan turned his weapon on the closest gunman and burned him down with a burst to the belly. As he folded, Bolan took down the man behind him. The BXP tripped off two more bursts and two more traitors fell, dead. Bolan's weapon clacked open on empty. The man with the shotgun snapped his weapon shut on two fresh shells. Bolan went for his Beretta, but the twin, gaping 10-gauge barrels rose for Bolan's face.

A shotgun roared from the doorway, and the killer's head snapped back in a red mist. Yotuel leaned heavily against the door with his weapon oozing smoke. *"Pinches cabrones..."*

The man holding the judge against the wall appeared to be frozen in shock. Judge Honore was whimpering. Bolan gazed at the prisoner. "Naida?"

"Sí!" The young woman burst into tears. *"Sí!"*

"Are you all right? Did they hurt you?"

Naida sobbed uncontrollably in her chains.

"Pol, you all right?"

He rose wearily to his feet. "Yeah."

"Call Roldan. Tell him we have his sister and she's all right." Bolan looked at the man holding the judge. "Keys. Now."

The dirty cop dropped the judge, who slid down the slimy wall to sit and weep, holding his face in his hands. The last dirty cop standing pointed at one of his fallen brethren. Bolan went through the dead man's pockets and found a set of giant iron keys. Naida flinched as he approached, but she calmed as Bolan smiled at her. "Let's get you out of here. Your brother misses you."

18

Both Roldan and his sister Naida had fallen to their knees in the kitchen and pressed their weeping faces against Bolan's hands. They thanked him, called upon a whole pantheon of saints to protect him, rattled out prayers, swore their eternal debt, soaked his sleeves with their tears of gratitude and then cycled through it again. Ola the maid sobbed in the background.

It took an effort, but Bolan hauled Roldan and his sister back to their feet. "Roldan, we need to put Naida and Ola someplace safe. We've burned most CIA safe assets in San Juan except for the station itself, and it's being watched. I don't want to pick up a tail. Anyone got a place we can take her?"

The Puerto Rican cops all looked at one another.

Yotuel d'Nico's voice rumbled. "The last place your enemies would look for Officer Roldan's sister would be among *La Neta*."

It wasn't the worst idea Bolan had ever heard. "The gangs would give her sanctuary?"

"If I tell them to." The Lion nodded.

Bolan looked to Roldan. "Can you live with that?"

Roldan snuffled and wiped his eyes. "Yes."

Bolan nodded. "Naida?"

"Yes. I'm not scared. I will do what you say."

"Good. Yotuel, make the call. I've got to make a call myself."

Blancanales followed Bolan into the tiny den, where he flipped open his laptop and punched some keys. Aaron Kurtzman appeared on the inset screen.

"Well, I've got your most likely minisubmarine route," Kurtzman announced.

"I was hoping you'd say that."

"The Caribbean is a whole lot deeper than most people think. The Venezuelan Basin between South America and Puerto Rico drops deeper than five thousand yards. Too deep for a minisubmersible to dive and too wide to sail across without days of exposure to ocean traffic and satellites."

"But?" Bolan inquired.

"But…" Kurtzman clicked up an oceanographic map of the Caribbean. "You go a bit eastward along Venezuela's coast and you've got the Isla de Margarita, and just north of that, bingo! The Aves Sea Ridge runs in an almost straight five-hundred-mile shot to the Virgin Islands. From there it's just a hop, skip and a jump to Puerto Rico. Some parts of the Aves Sea Ridge are less than twenty-three yards below the surface. That's periscope depth for any minisub with caterpillar treads we have specs on. They can crawl from seamount to seamount, and all along that ridge you have islands that are little more than specks of rock. A few are a bit larger, and interestingly enough several of them are owned or claimed by Venezuela. Crawling along the bottom at periscope depth, the subs would be very hard to detect, and that assumes anyone is actively looking for them. Fact is, Mack, they could have been staging this coup for months, maybe even a year or more, and we'd be none the wiser."

"Bear, you're a genius," Bolan concluded.

"I know I am. But it was your idea, and now we need proof. The President is going to quietly put the Puerto Rican coast guard on the lookout around the eastern coast of the island."

Bolan shook his head. "No. I think best case the coast guard is being monitored, worst case they've been infiltrated or key people bought off. If the Venezuelans even get the ghost of an idea that we're on to them and patrolling, they'll cease all clandestine insertions. We want them caught red-handed."

"All right. No coast guard." Kurtzman typed some more keys. "You'll have to break something open on your end."

"Well, the good news is Pol's been having epiphanies 24/7." Bolan clicked some keys of his own and sent a map to Kurtzman. "He wanted to organize a little hunting party on Vieques Island until we got sidetracked."

Kurtzman's brows bunched as he pulled up geographical stats. "You know, Vieques isn't bad."

"The population is only about ten thousand, only two major towns, depressed economy, you wouldn't have to spread much money around to get the keys to the kingdom. They could have their own firebase down there and no one would be the wiser."

Bolan scrutinized the map of Vieques. "I'm going to have to assume they own the island or anything on it that's near them. They'll have paid off the local cops and have eyes watching the airport and private landing strips. My team is pretty smashed up and only Pol and I are jump-qualified. I'm going to need a boat for a clandestine insertion, preferably a catamaran with as shallow a draft as possible."

Kurtzman liked it. "I can have Barb arrange the boat ASAP."

"Good. I want to set sail at dawn and hit Vieques by nightfall. Meanwhile, I want satellite on the island. Find me any kind of suspicious movement, anything at all, and see if you can work up a list of most likely locations the enemy might be using."

"On it. Bear out."

EIGHT HOURS OF SLEEP and the bracing ocean wind had done the team wonders. The catamaran was tip-top and loaded to the gills with weapons and gear. Bolan looked over his team as the sun set. Constante had lost a finger and his best friend. Gustolallo had a concussion from the ax attack. Unda's shirtless torso was crisscrossed with lacerations. Blancanales's chest looked like he'd been beaten with a baseball bat. Bolan shook his head as he looked at the Lion. Yotuel looked like a dead man looking for a grave to fall into. Roldan had been in half a dozen firefights in half as many days and there wasn't a scratch on him. He seemed to have a halo over his head.

The soldier gave himself a critical self-survey.

Since he'd arrived in Puerto Rico, he'd been attacked with everything from battle-axes to flamethrowers and most forms of handheld weapons in between. Besides some stitches, singed eyebrows and an injured left hand, he was pretty much living on borrowed time. Bolan's smile faded. The problem was luck always ran out.

And Bolan had a bad feeling about the island of Vieques.

Yotuel limped across to the center hull where Bolan held the wheel.

"Amigo, give me a pistol. Something big."

Bolan kept his eyes on the looming purple landmass of Vieques. "Pol already gave you a rifle, a nice one."

"I know…but my left hand." Yotuel held up a huge paw that shook as it failed to make a fist. "It's gone weak."

Bolan drew his Beretta 93-R and pushed the selector switch to three-round burst. "This is my personal favorite."

Yotuel took the machine pistol in his right hand and

admired the extra bit of barrel and folded strut of the foregrip beneath the slide. *"Gracias."*

Bolan filled a ditty bag with ten spare magazines and held it out. *"De nada."*

The Lion's remaining eye stared at Bolan unblinkingly as he draped the ammo over his shoulder. The right corner of his mouth turned up and his left struggled to follow suit. "I'm fucked up, aren't I?"

Bolan measured the Lion in honest appraisal. He'd seen these symptoms before. Bolan shrugged. "You're bleeding inside the brain. The pressure is building up. You're going to die."

Yotuel's split-faced smile stayed painted on his face. "Then put this tub on the beach *pronto* and find me some *venezolanos* to shoot at."

"You got it."

Yotuel stumbled back to the bow with his new weapon. Blancanales shot Bolan a questioning look. "What was all that about?"

Bolan shook his head. "He's fading fast."

"Jesus."

"He volunteered, Pol. He's made his choice."

Blancanales gazed at the oncoming island and changed the subject. "The Bear able to find anything for us?"

"Well, the U.S. Navy used Vieques as a firing range and a weapons testing ground from World War II right up until 2003. Protests shut the ranges down but there are still observation towers, shacks and other facilities for the ground assessment teams that are still standing. The Bear found a little facility right on the coast. It's been closed for years now, but it has everything your minisub infiltrators could want—a pier, a boat shed, a gas pump, a helicopter pad and some abandoned prefab shacks."

"And if anyone noticed anything out of the ordinary, they're trained infiltrators. They could just say they are part of a cleanup crew and be treated like heroes." Blancanales sighed. "For that matter, this is Latin America. They could just pose as smugglers, spread some money around and let it be known they'll kill anyone who talks."

"Or they just say they're *Macheteros*. The Viequenses have a long-standing grudge against the mainland for the 'military occupation' and the destruction of the sugar industry here."

"So it looks like an idyllic infiltration getaway." Blancanales scratched his chin. "But what makes this one special?"

"An anomaly."

"What kind of anomaly?"

Bolan clicked on a jpeg file. "What do you make of that?"

Blancanales peered at a photograph taken by an NSA high-resolution, infrared imaging satellite. It appeared to be two parallel troughs against a blank background. "Looks like tracks from a tracked vehicle."

"Yeah."

"Yeah, but if this was a bombing and weapons-testing facility, they would have had bulldozers." Blancanales frowned. "I bet there are dozens of such tracks at the facility."

"There are. But these tracks are on the beach and above the tidal line." Bolan clicked on another file that showed nothing. "And tonight they're gone."

"Well, wind and the daily downpour might explain that." Blancanales's teeth flashed. "Or…"

"Or someone's been sweeping up after themselves," Bolan concluded. He turned to the rest of the team. "Gear up. We're going to hit the target area within the hour."

19

Isla de Vieques

"Looks quiet," Blancanales observed.

"Yeah." Bolan scanned the ghost facility through the optics of his FN SCAR rifle.

They had docked the catamaran about a half mile down the beach and crept along the tree line toward the little facility. They watched the compound now. The pier and the boathouse looked abandoned. Turning to Blancanales, Bolan said, "You and I are going in for a closer look. Inspector, we may be coming back in a hurry, so stay sharp."

"Yes." The inspector held up his Thompson. "We will be ready."

"Let's do it." Bolan and Blancanales loped through the palm trees that fringed the edge of the beach. They crossed the little one-lane road that cut through the palms and led to the gate. Both men stopped again. Storm fencing topped with razor wire guarded the perimeter, and the palm groves had been pushed back a hundred yards in an arc around the facility. Blancanales spoke quietly. "One wonders why a naval observation, support and cleanup facility would need a kill zone."

Bolan slung his rifle on his back. "Cover me."

He dropped to the ground and began to crawl between the palm stumps. It was pathetic cover at best. He stopped

as he reached the perimeter fence, reached into his web
bear and pulled out a black plastic box the size of a garage-
door opener. He deployed two small antennae and touched
them to the fence. The readout showed no current running
through the fence and no circuit to break. Bolan held up a
hand and waved forward Blancanales, who then signaled
Constante and the Puerto Rican team to move up.

Bolan pulled his shears and started parting links of the
fence. He had just about a two-foot, half-moon of fence cut
when he heard Blancanales's breathing and the crunch of
knees and elbows grinding the sand.

The slice of fence barely chinked as Bolan eased it
down but it sounded loud enough to wake the dead. "I'm
going in. Cover me."

There was a tiny scrape and rattle of gear as Blancanales
deployed his rifle. "Go."

Bolan hunched a hairbreadth beneath the jagged prongs
of cut fence. He rolled to his feet and ran ten yards to put
himself in the shadow and dubious cover of a portable
toilet. Blancanales's voice spoke in his earpiece. "What do
you think?"

"I got nada." Bolan scanned the facility grounds. "But
I feel them. They're here."

Bolan ran another fifteen yards and put his back to a
Quonset hut. He put his ear to the corrugated iron but there
was no sound inside. "Pol, come ahead. Inspector, move
your team up to the fence."

Blancanales's boots crunched sand as he moved up to
Bolan's last position. "On your six."

More agonizing moments passed as Constante moved
his team up. "We're at the fence," the inspector said.

Bolan scanned the tiny ghost town. "Copy that."

Constante whispered across the link. "Yotuel's fading."

"Yeah," Bolan replied. "I know." The one-hundred-yard crawl wouldn't have done the dying man any favors. "Pol, move up. Inspector, cover him."

Blancanales loped up to the hut and crouched beside Bolan. "Okay, where the hell are they?"

"I don't know. I'd say tunnels, but they would have to be big. Satellite imaging showed no signs of dredging or construction in the water off the beach. They've built a firebase with nothing in it."

"Quonset huts could hide minisubs."

Bolan shook his head. "Show me the door you could drive them through."

"A crane could lift them up and drop them back down if they'd been gutted."

"I don't see a crane." Bolan lifted his chin at one of the hut's tiny windows. "But we saw tracks. Do it."

Blancanales's knife rasped from its sheath and he jimmied the window with professional ease. He gingerly set the pane down and shook his head. "Nothing but empty bunks."

Bolan trained his optics past the free-fire zone beyond the fence. The palm forest gave way to tropical trees and it was dark beneath them—too dark for a single level of tree canopy. "Pol, what do you make of that?"

Blancanales trained his rifle's scope on the inland expanse of Vieques Island. "That's either some funky undergrowth or there's camouflage netting in the forest."

Bolan saw the same thing. "They're not in the naval facility." He scanned through his optics. He didn't see anything, but he felt the enemy like a lurking force. "They're in the trees." He scanned the perimeter and saw two fence support posts set inches away from each other. "That's the gate. The subs come in off the beach and go right through into the shelter of the forest. See it?"

"Oh, I see it."

Bolan spoke into his mike. "Inspector, move your team into the compound. Roldan, I want you to go check the pumps and the boathouse. We'll cover you."

"*Sí,* Cooper." Roldan ran, ducking from building to building to keep the sheds and huts between himself and the unnaturally dark forest behind the facility. The tension mounted while they waited. Roldan came back breathlessly across the link. "Cooper! The boathouse is empty! There are no locks on the pumps. They have two fuel tanks, one for gasoline and one for diesel. Both are at least half-full."

"Copy that, Roldan."

"Wait!" Panic crept into Roldan's voice. "Coop! I—"

"What is it Roldan?"

"Shit!"

Bolan shook his head as a generator kicked into life in the boathouse.

"Coop!" Roldan was appalled. "I didn't turn that on!"

The young cop had tripped some kind of alarm. Bolan could hear the snap and hum of power in the lines. He yanked up his goggles just as the facility lit up under the harsh glare of klieg lights. Blancanales sighed. "Here it comes."

Automatic weapons began opening up from the darkness beneath the trees. Bolan flipped up the ladder sight for his grenade launcher and exchanged a high-explosive round for the frag. "Roldan."

"I'm sorry, Coop! I don't know what I did! I—"

"Roldan!" Bolan snarled.

"What?"

"Jump."

"What?"

Bolan aimed his weapon at the boathouse and Roldan. "Jump."

"Shit!" Roldan took five running steps down the wooden pier and hurled himself into the lagoon. Bolan fired his weapon. The grenade spiraled across the compound and sailed through the open boathouse door. The interior flashed orange as the grenade detonated, and the compound fell beneath a comforting blanket of darkness as the murdered generator stopped pumping juice.

"Roldan." Bolan pulled down his goggles and jacked in a frag round as rifle fire continued to rake the compound from the trees. "Roldan, you all right?"

Roldan coughed up seawater on the other side of the link. "*Sí*, Coop."

"Good. Link up." Bolan and Blancanales lobbed grenades toward the trees as Roldan wove his way back to the team.

Blancanales was counting flashes in the dark. "I put them at about squad strength."

Bolan saw it the same way. "This isn't a firebase! It's an infiltration hub! Personnel will be minimal! We should—" Bolan's eyes widened beneath his goggles. "Crap."

The much-theorized minisubmersibles came rolling out of the trees. They were about the size of a pair of humpback whales, but instead of fins they had tank treads and instead of a hump they had a submarine sail.

The two behemoths wallowed forward across the empty kill zone, crushing palm stumps. The men in the sails opened up with their DShK heavy machine guns. They were using their tracked submersibles like armored fighting vehicles. Bolan and his team had nothing more solid than prefab sheds for cover, and nothing in their arsenal that could crack the pressure hull of a submarine. Tracers streaked through the walls of the Quonset hut as if they were tissue paper.

Bolan looked at Blancanales. "I don't suppose you brought the LAW rockets?"

Blancanales shrugged. They had brought along limpet mines to disable any minisubmarines they found, but by their nature someone would have to walk up, attach the mines by hand and arm them. Bolan suspected the gunners in the sails would take a dim view of anyone who tried that. Bolan pulled a discus-shaped mine from his pack. Someone was going to have to try anyway. "Damn."

Yotuel's voice slurred behind Bolan. "Hey, Cooper."

Bolan glanced back at him. The left side of Yotuel's mouth was sagging and drooling. The right half was grinning as he held up a Russian RKG-3 antitank grenade. "You beat me up with this in the alley, and when you and your friend were on the computer, I went through your bags to find it. I had hoped to return the favor when this was all over." The Lion flipped the grenade in his hand and held it out to Bolan handle first. "But now I would rather see you return the favor to these *venezolanos* for what they have done to my island."

Bolan accepted the antiarmor weapon. "You've redeemed yourself."

The Lion's smile was a horrible inverted *s* in the dark. "You will need a diversion."

Gustolallo's voice broke. "Yotuel; no!"

The two subs crushed the perimeter fencing beneath their treads and entered the compound.

Yotuel kept his eye on Bolan. "I'm going to count to ten."

Bolan nodded. The Lion was making his stand. "Start counting. Pol, with me." Bolan rose and began running around the rear of the hut. Blancanales's boots pounded sand behind him. Bolan counted as he ran. He turned the corner on the hut as he reached ten.

The Lion lurched into the open and roared his defiance. *"Boricuas!"* He raised the Beretta 93-R and began firing bursts as fast as he could pull the trigger. Trios of sparks whined off the closer minisub. DShK heavy machine guns swiveled on their mounts toward the *La Neta* lord. Yotuel fired off his seventh and last burst, and the Beretta clacked open on an empty chamber. The Lion stood before the oncoming behemoths and slammed the empty machine pistol over his heart again and again in solidarity for the island of his birth. *"Boricuas* forever! *Siempre! Siempre! Siem—"*

The Russian heavy machine guns shredded the Lion where he stood.

The blast of the crew-served weapons and Yotuel's stand blinded the gunners to Bolan's advance for a few fatal heartbeats. Bolan pulled the pin on the RKG-3 grenade and hurled the bomb high. It landed just in front of the closer sub's sail and detonated. Smoke and yellow fire flashed. The machine gunner screamed as superheated gas erupted from the hatch into the tiny one-man sail and seared the lower half of his body. Minisubs had only one main chamber. The shaped charge warhead of the grenade would have turned the crew compartment into a kiln. The sub ground to a halt on its tracks, and the machine gun fell limp on its mount as the charred gunner screamed and fell flailing in the sail.

"Pol! Cover me!" Bolan roared.

Blancanales stopped, dropped to one knee, and raised his rifle. The grenade launcher beneath the barrel thudded and the gunner in the second sub had the good sense to drop and let the shrapnel splash against the rolled steel of the sail. Blancanales started firing bursts from his rifle. Bolan dropped his own rifle as he reached the stricken sub and jumped. He put his foot on the caterpillar track's fairing and vaulted up to grab the edge of the sail. The burned gunner screamed as Bolan vaulted on top of him into the sail. Bolan ignored him and put his hands on the spade grips of the machine gun and tracked it around on its ring mount. The machine gunner in the other sub had suddenly become aware of the situation. He ignored Blancanales's incoming fire and swung his weapon back online to cut Bolan apart.

Bolan pressed both thumbs on the paddle trigger and fired.

The DShK bucked and shuddered on its mount. Bolan destroyed the other sub's sail with over fifty rounds. The enemy gunner twisted and fell limp over his machine gun. Bolan swung his weapon around and held his trigger down, ripping the rest of his ammo belt in an arc into the tree line. "Inspector! Pol and I are going to take the other sub! We need covering fire!"

Constante, Gustolallo, Roldan and Unda rose from their flimsy cover and began firing their weapons.

"Pol!" Bolan boomed. "Go!"

Blancanales charged the second sub. Bolan abandoned his spent machine gun and leaped into space. His boots hit sand and the shock slammed up his spine. He drew his .50-caliber Desert Eagle pistol and crouched by the side of the rained submersible. Bullets whined off the hull as enemy riflemen sought him. Bolan dropped to one knee. A man had popped up in the sail of the other craft and was shoving aside his dead comrade to get to the machine gun as Blancanales charged. Bolan took aim and fired. The would-be machine gunner toppled over the back of the sail and slid toward the sand. Whoever was driving slammed the sub into Reverse, but Blancanales was already upon them. He swung up the side of the sub and dropped a hand grenade down the sail's open hatch.

The sub ground to a halt as the cramped interior turned into a meat grinder of whizzing and ricocheting shrapnel.

Blancanales dropped his rifle, pulled his pistol and went down the hatch. His .45 cut loose three times within the hull. Increasing fire was coming out of the trees. Bolan charged through the cross fire and pulled himself up into the sail as bullets from the trees sparked off the hull. He yanked open the DShK's feed cover and slapped in a fresh belt. Bolan shouted down the sail. "Pol! Get this tub moving!"

"Working on it!" Blancanales snarled. The Able Team warrior shoved his face into the pilot's periscope hood. He stepped on the gas as he pulled his right handle back and rammed the left forward. The sub's engine whined and yowled in response, and the submersible slowly spun on its axis.

Bolan was already working. Palm trees and dry-forest deciduous trees were no cover against a heavy machine gun, and Bolan raked the darkness and reaped the muzzle-blast of anyone who fired back. Constante shouted across the line. "We're coming forward!"

"Do it!" The heavy machine gun hammered on its mount as Bolan continued to spray cheroot-sized bullets on full-auto. Constante and crew charged out of the compound and fell in behind to use the bulk of the sub for cover.

Blancanales shouted from below as he rolled the sub back across the free-fire zone. "Hit the spotlight!"

Bolan flipped up the spotlight on its post and aimed it forward. Armed men scrambled beneath the netting. Men tore off their night-vision equipment as their goggles amplified the spotlight to blinding proportions or solarized with light overload. The sub lumbered forward.

Constante, Unda, Roldan and Gustolallo fanned out two by two on either side of the sub, walking forward in a skirmish line with their guns blazing. The headlights of an old army jeep glared back as the vehicle came tearing out from beneath a tarp. Bolan slewed his front sight around onto the hood and put a burst through the engine block. The jeep swerved wildly and hit a tree. The driver folded in two around the steering column with the impact while the passenger went through the windshield and hit the tree facefirst with a sickening crunch.

The forest camp was suddenly very quiet. Bolan took the opportunity to load a fresh belt of ammo into the smoking heavy machine gun. He called out to the Puerto Ricans. "Sweep the camp. I'll cover you from here."

Constante and the crew began picking through the camp with the thoroughness of cops at a crime scene. "Got a live one!" Unda called out. Roldan knelt over a man. "Another one! Here!"

Gustolallo waved wildly. "Coop! You need to see this!"

"Pol, take the gun. Cover us." Bolan dismounted and went over to where Gustolallo stood.

Bolan gazed down at the wounded man. A burst from the Russian heavy machine gun had cleanly ripped his legs off at the knees. Many Venezuelans were of pure aboriginal Indian blood, and it gave them a characteristic, vaguely Asiatic look. The man under Gustolallo's gun was Asiatic, but he wasn't of Venezuelan *indio* ethnicity. He was very clearly Chinese. Bolan spoke in his limited Mandarin.

"Good evening, comrade."

The legless man jerked at the sound of his native language.

Bolan smiled thinly and switched to English. "Let's not screw around. If you're training Venezuelan commandos to penetrate Latin American and Caribbean targets, you speak Spanish and English."

The Chinese agent bit his lower lip.

"Listen, let's make this quick. As far as I'm concerned

you're a terrorist, an infiltrator, a spy and you have no rights under the U.S. Constitution."

The Chinese man started to sweat.

"I'm not going to torture you," Bolan continued. "I'm not into that. But what I will do is leave you here with no legs for the ghost crabs and the gulls. I'm going to leave you to the scavengers without the benefit of morphine."

The man looked like he was about to bite his lip through. Bolan had no doubt the man was tough, but the combination of being crippled and captured often had a very demoralizing short-term effect on men of action.

"If you cooperate, I will see that you receive medical attention and access to the Chinese consulate." Bolan shrugged affably. "Should you fear the rewards for failure from your government, I am prepared to promise you that in return for your cooperation the U.S. government will give you full medical rehabilitation, asylum and a new identity and relocation. Make your choice."

Tears spilled out of the Chinese agent's eyes. Crippled incarceration or ending up carrion food would be the only rewards for his defiance.

Bolan prodded the agent's thought process along. "American prosthetic technology is among the best in the world. If you cooperate, you will walk again. You have information the United States government wants. But if you're going to help me," Bolan concluded, "you have to do it now."

20

"What shape is the sub in?" Bolan asked.

"There's minor shrapnel damage all around the crew compartment, but it's mostly cosmetic and nothing that will interfere with running the boat," Blancanales said. "We've refueled and recharged the batteries and resupplied it with food, water and weapons. We consolidated the ammo for the heavy machine guns, and you've got three belts. Overall? I'm calling her tip-top. You and I can both handle a boat, so barring any heavy weather we should be able to sail her on the surface no problem. If we use the tracks on the bottom, it's just like driving a tank—though I expect navigating on the bottom will be interesting. You want to dive deep? Things are going to get interesting real fast."

The sub had been shot hundreds of times, hit with grenades and the sail looked like the surface of the moon. None of it was critical, but Bolan had no desire to take her down deep to see if she had lost any structural integrity. "How'd you do with the torpedoes?"

In many ways the team had been very lucky. They'd found crates for RPGs in the camp, but they were empty and hadn't been used against them. Most likely the weapons had already been distributed to the cells on Puerto Rico's main island. Bolan's assessment had been correct. The facility on Vieques had been an infiltration and distribution hub. They had found about a hundred M-16 rifles and ammo that had yet to be handed out, and a significant cache of C-4 high explosives. The most interesting find had been four Russian APR-2 antisubmarine acoustic homing torpedoes beneath a tarp. The infiltrators were apparently prepared to sink a few things to get the revolution up to speed.

"We got the launch racks attached to the sides of the hull. I'll need another half an hour to run the electrical connections out through the tread fairings, and then I'll need everybody's help winching the torpedoes into place. Call it an hour before we can roll her out to sea."

"Nice work," Bolan said.

Blancanales looked back toward the trees where the legless Chinese was resting comfortably in a hammock. "How did you do with our friend?"

"His name is Kao Chu-Chieh, lieutenant, Chinese special purpose adviser. He's from the PRC's newly formed Americas Division. He's cooperating for immunity, and I've since given him first aid and got him morphined to the gills. I had him check in over his satellite rig with Caracas. Unless he's a better poker player than I am, everything seems copacetic. We should have a twenty-four-hour window before anyone suspects anything is wrong. Plus these guys are infiltrators. If something goes wrong, they're supposed to go dark and escape and evade rather than call for help. Kao gave me the latest call signs and code words. We might just have a smooth shot at the target."

"Yeah, and what's our target?" Blancanales asked.

"Isla Aves," Bolan replied.

"Island of Birds?"

"Bear looked it up. It's occupied by Venezuela, but the claim is disputed by Dominica. The island is about three hundred and seventy-five yards long, fifty yards wide and about four yards above sea level on a calm day. It's a resting and mating ground for migrating seabirds and turtles. The Venezuelans built a scientific naval base there in 1978. There's a light and radio tower, a radar unit and a small Venezuelan coast-guard station. The real interesting thing is that according to Bear the Venezuelans expanded the station in 2004. Particularly the coast-guard base part of it built over the water on stilts."

"Well, that sounds like their submarine dock." Blancanales nodded. "And Isla Aves is their untouchable sovereign-soil transport point."

"That's the way I figure it."

Blancanales rapped his knuckles against the minisub's hull. "And you want to sail this pig out across the Caribbean and to this island?"

"Yep. Isla Aves is about two hundred miles southeast of here."

Blancanales did some math. "This sub is a pig, Mack. Those treads and their fairings create a hell of a lot of drag, and the torpedoes are going to add even more. I doubt she'll do much more than twenty knots on the surface and that's throttles full forward, and like I said, she isn't made for open-ocean sailing. She was designed for clandestine crawling."

There was no getting around it. They were in for a very bumpy twenty-four-hour ride. "Pol, let's do it."

Bolan turned as Roldan walked up to them. He was sweating through his T-shirt and he had a shovel in his hand. "What's up, amigo?"

"Gustolallo and I buried Yotuel."

Bolan nodded. "Good."

Roldan stared at his feet. "We thought you might say some words."

"All right." Bolan followed Roldan back to the forest camp. Blancanales knocked on the hull and Constante and

Unda emerged. There was a quick conversation in Spanish
and they followed. Gustolallo stood at the edge of the
forest leaning on a spade with a bandana pressed against
her wounded buttock. Roldan had chosen a flat bit of
ground where the sand had given way to soil. There was
hardly any mound. Yotuel d'Nico had been a big man, but
Roldan and Gustolallo had dug deep. The only marker was
a two-foot-long conquistador lance blade stabbed into the
ground at the head of the grave. It was laced with the
Lion's and *La Neta* beads. Everyone bowed their heads.

Bolan took a long breath and considered the eulogy.

Yotuel "the Lion" d'Nico was a gang lord and a convicted
felon. Yotuel would know that there would be no saving
grace for his soul, nor redemption for his crimes against his
people and against humanity. His place in hell was assured.
Bolan stood over the final resting place of a murdering,
drug-dealing, pimping, leg-breaking extortionist. Yet, in the
last minutes of his life, the Lion had added patriot and hero
to his résumé. Bolan gave the Lion the last benediction. The
only thing to be said about him was the truth. "Yotuel died
for Puerto Rico. He died going forward." Bolan let his breath
out. "He died *Boricua*. He's not going to have died in vain."

Bolan turned and started walking back to the sub. "Get
the winches up. I want the torpedoes loaded, and I want to
be sailing before dawn."

Isla Aves

Isla Aves lay dead ahead. The engine overheating had
forced them to throttle back and it had taken nearly forty-
eight hours to sail the two hundred miles from Vieques.

Bolan peered into the periscope. Isla Aves was just about
the loneliest sandbar Bolan had ever seen. It was literally

in the middle of nowhere. It lived up to the description Kurtzman had given him. The lighthouse, if it could be called that, was a skeletal tower of bare girders with a tiny roofed platform and a radio antenna mounted on top. A little ways away a small concrete building squatted in the sand with a radar dish on top. Bolan swiveled the scope onto the Venezuelan naval base. "Base" was a pretty grandiose name for what looked like a couple of gas stations on stilts. The platform was solid enough to have a crane mounted over the pier and there was a pumping station beneath it. About half was above water and the other half over the beach. An armed, twenty-five-foot, American-made Guardian patrol speedboat lay at dock.

Bolan noted a pair of men standing by the crane smoking and enjoying the late-afternoon breeze. Neither man was in Venezuelan coast guard uniform. Both men carried Kalashnikov rifles.

Constante turned from the communications console. "We are being hailed."

Roldan's head snapped around. "How?"

Bolan had factored in being detected. "The Venezuelan navy must have emplaced passive listening sonar buoys around the seamount when they did their 2004 expansion. They probably heard our screw noise as we came in."

Blancanales flipped open the notebook that had the latest codes and call signs. "So you want me to answer?"

"You're going to have to if we're going to get in range."

Pol took the headset from Constante and began to spin lies over the radio. There had been trouble on Vieques. Puerto Rican main-island authorities knew something had been going on at the closed U.S. naval gunnery facility. All infiltration agents had dispersed into the hills and gone dark. Local police in their pay had been instructed to plant the story that the abandoned facility was being used as a transshipment point by suspected Colombian drug smugglers. Both subs had successfully set sail without detection. Sub number two was having engine difficulties and was some hours behind.

Long awkward moments passed as all of this was digested. Blancanales's brows bunched. "We're being ordered to surface and come ahead slow."

"Acknowledge and do it."

Blancanales pressed a button to release ballast and the minisub slowly rose. Bolan pressed a button and the periscope retracted. "Surfaced," he said.

"Inspector, get on the periscope. Keep an eye on things. Let's move ahead slowly," Bolan said.

The engine whined into life, and Blancanales pushed his controls forward. Bolan clambered up the tiny ladder and spun the hatch open. The sea air was like a blessing from God. The heavy machine gun had been strapped down up top for quick mounting and spent forty-eight hours in the salt and spray. Bolan spritzed the action with a can of machine oil and slapped in a belt of ammo.

Bolan's blood froze as he heard tube noise from the base.

Constante shouted up the hatch. "Coop! I saw a puff of smoke!"

The enemy had mortars, and by the sound they were 120 mm or larger. Bolan dropped down out of the sail and slammed the hatch down. "Dive! Dive! Dive!"

The good news was that with its tractor treads and thousand-pound torpedoes mounted on either side of the hull, the little sub desperately wanted to sink like a stone. The other good news was that mortars flung their ordinance up in huge arcs and they had a lot of hang time. The bad news was that the sub's torpedoes were externally mounted. It wouldn't take too much of a shock wave to set them off.

The blast wave from the 120 mm mortar warhead rolled through the minisub like a slap. Everyone held their breath. The torpedoes didn't detonate, but Gustolallo shrieked as water spritzed her from a compromised seal in the hatch. Blancanales shouted as the passive sonar gave him ugly news. "I have engine noise! That patrol boat just fired up her diesels!"

Bolan raised the periscope. "Torpedo number one! Activate acoustic sensors!"

Blancanales flipped a switch on his primitive weapon console. "Torpedo number one! Acoustic sensor active! Target acquired!"

"Fire torpedo!"

"Firing torpedo!" Blancanales punched the Fire button and the sub lurched as the torpedo left the launch rack and she suddenly became a thousand pounds unbalanced on her port side. "Torpedo away!" Blancanales fought the controls to bring the minisub back in trim. "Jesus…"

The periscope broke the surface. The patrol boat was just moving away from dock. The torpedo surfaced like a gray blur and knifed toward the accelerating patrol boat like a shark.

"Direct hit! Bring her to the surface!" Bolan said

The Executioner lined up the periscope's crosshairs with the axis of the sub as they surfaced. "Twenty degrees to starboard!"

"Twenty degrees to starboard!" The sub slowly turned in the water. They would have only a few seconds before the mortar spotter reacquired their position and the mortar team adjusted its aim. The nose of the sub achingly moved to aim at the darkness beneath the Venezuelan platform.

"All stop!" The crosshairs were dead on. "Torpedo number two, arm contact fuse and fire!"

"Torpedo number two, contact fuse armed! Fire!" Blancanales hit the fire control. "Torpedo away!"

Bolan tracked the torpedo as it flashed just below the surface. The bow-like wake it threw pointed straight at the Venezuelan base like an arrow. The torpedo disappeared beneath it and orange fire flashed. The water geyser smashed against the bottom of the platform and channeled out from under it in all directions like a ruptured pressure cooker. "Direct hit!"

The Puerto Ricans cheered.

There was a sudden second and much larger third explosion. The platform sagged on its stilts, and thick black smoke followed the maelstrom of displaced water. It seemed the Venezuelan infiltrators had been hiding things beneath the platform they didn't want any prying satellites overhead to see.

"Significant secondary explosions," Bolan stated. The little pier and the pumping station remained remarkably intact. He stood wide-legged before the periscope. "Engage the caterpillar tracks. All ahead full. Ramming speed."

Blancanales grinned as he shoved his controls forward and flipped on the drive for the treads. He was really starting to enjoy this. "Yes, sir, Captain!"

"Steady on, steady on, steady on…" Bolan turned to the rest of his shipmates. "Brace for impact!"

Everyone grabbed for racks and cleats and anything bolted down.

The minisub smashed into the pier at a little over twenty knots. Wood snapped in all directions. Pilings cracked and shattered as the sub's multiton momentum took it through the wooden structure. Bolan's feet went out from under him as the sub hit sand at full speed and the lights went out. He hung for a moment by the periscope handles and a body went flying past him. Red emergency lights clicked on, and Blancanales fought the bucking controls. It was a miracle they hadn't thrown a track.

"Welcome to Bird Island!" Blancanales shouted. "The eagle has landed!"

They were on land.

"Inspector!" Bolan threw open the hatch and heaved himself up into the sail. "With me!"

Constante clambered up behind him, and they manhandled the heavy machine gun onto its mount. Constante shoved in the retaining pin, and Bolan racked the action on a live round. He swung the weapon around on its mount to aim behind them. The mutilated pumping station was ribboning amber diesel fuel into the air like a park fountain. Bolan squeezed his trigger and sent a stream of armor-piercing incendiary bullets into the pumps. Flames began crawling among the wreckage, and Bolan was suddenly rewarded with a thump as the tanks below ignited. What remained of the pier disappeared in the fireball, and a little mushroom cloud of smoke and fire rose into the air.

Constante lit a cigarette and sighed happily. "Beautiful work."

"Thanks." Bolan called down the hatch. "Unda! Roldan! Get your gear!"

The platform was sagging and on fire, but some men were still trying to lay rifle fire on the sub. Bolan fired suppressive bursts while Unda and Roldan squeezed up into the sail and then leaped to the sand with bags full of the C-4 they had found on Vieques. The two cops ran up to the radar bunker. Roldan pulled his fuse and hurled it up into the cup of the radar dish. Three seconds later the radar dish and its support equipment were scraped from the top of the building in smoke and fire. The force of the blast sat Roldan down in the sand. Unda kicked in the door and shouted to any occupants that the next charge was going inside.

A pair of men in white, Venezuelan naval uniform blouses and shorts bolted from the building and ran for their lives. Unda pulled the fuse on his satchel charge and heaved it inside the little bunker. He yanked Roldan up to his feet as the thick storm windows blew out and smoke belched out the open door. Bolan called down the hatch with sudden inspiration. "Gustolallo! Give me the red bag!"

Gustolallo handed up a small and very heavy red bag that clanked. Bolan took out the four discus-shaped objects and began adjusting timers while Roldan and Unda joined him. Roldan beamed. "We did it!"

Bolan pointed back behind them. "You forgot the tower."

Unda stared in confusion. "But Cooper, we have no more C-4!"

Bolan slid the four weapons back in the red bag. "You're forgetting the limpet mines."

Roldan looked like he might burst into flames with happiness.

Bolan tossed the bag to Roldan. "One on each post. They're magnetic, so just strip the back cover, slap it on, and then push the green button twice. I set the timers for fifteen seconds."

Roldan and Unda divvied up the mines and ran back for the radio tower. They stripped the covers and slapped the mines one apiece to each tower support and reached the sub in time to watch. The limpet mines cracked like bullwhips as they detonated, and their shaped charges sheared through the supports like hot knives. The tower buckled and then toppled like a giant tree of iron. Unda and Roldan pumped their fists and cheered.

Bolan kept his weapon trained on the burning platform. Many of the men on it had jumped into the water, and now they were slogging up onto the beach. The two radar operators stood around looking lost. "Inspector, ask them how many naval personnel are on the platform."

Constante spoke quietly with the two sailors. "They say just them. They are needed to operate the radar."

"Ask who's manning the platform."

"They say they do not know, and they are not supposed to ask," Constante replied.

"What about the scientists that are permanently stationed here?"

Constante smiled. "They say the marine biology team was sent home months ago."

Bolan jerked his head at Roldan and Unda. "Mount up." The two cops clambered up the side and dropped down the hatch. Bolan called to Blancanales. "Bring us up to where the survivors are congregating."

The tracks clanked and whined and the sub began crawling across the sand. About twenty men were milling on the shore. They flinched as Bolan fired a burst into the sand in front of them. The men who were still armed got the message and dropped their rifles and pistols. The survivors jumped as a unit as the mortar bombs on the burning platform began detonating in a series of thunderclaps. It was the last straw for the beleaguered base. Structurally compromised concrete and steel supports cracked and tore and the entire base tipped and fell like it had been kneecapped. The platform came to rest in the shallow water like a ship run aground.

Bolan nodded at his handiwork. "That should just about do it."

Constante took a long meditative drag on his cigarette. "I think you are forgetting something."

"Oh?" Bolan inquired.

"Yes. We are now officially at war with Venezuela."

"No, I don't think so. We have both Venezuelan and Chinese prisoners. I think the generals in Caracas are going to be quiet as church mice, take this one on the chin and pray we don't take any further action. They can't afford to have the United States boycott eighty percent of their oil production, and they sure as hell can't afford open war with us. They played a very dangerous game, and they lost. They're just going to have to suck it up and like it."

"Yes, but I am not totally confident that they won't try again."

"You know, I was just thinking the same thing," Bolan agreed. "Translate what I say exactly."

The sub ground to halt in front of the survivors. Bolan kept the muzzle of the heavy machine gun trained on the sodden, burned and dispirited men and raised his voice. "As you can see, I am aware of you! Tell your superiors that I am aware of you! Tell them I've destroyed many of your cells in Puerto Rico and I have taken prisoners! If they're smart, they will order the cells I haven't destroyed yet to disperse and return home! *La Neta* and the gangs know who and what you are and I've turned them against you! Your base on Vieques has been eliminated and the Chinese advisor there has been captured and is cooperating with me!"

Many of the Venezuelans visibly jerked and flinched like they were taking blows with each statement.

Bolan's voice dropped dangerously low. "Tell them if you come back to Puerto Rico—" he lifted his chin around at the burning and twisted devastation littering the island from one end to the other "—I'll be coming to Caracas."

Bolan thumped the floor of the sail. "Pol, take us out of here."

"You got it!" Blancanales called up.

The minisub rumbled down to the beach and hit the surf with a splash. Constante lit another cigarette and stared across the empty blue expanse. Blancanales called out what both Bolan and Constante were both thinking. "Hey! Skipper! I don't think we have the fuel to reach Puerto Rico! I don't think we can reach the Virgin Islands or anything else we own!"

Bolan consulted his mental map of the Caribbean. They needed someplace nice with friendly people who wouldn't mind a clandestine sub landing, someplace where Bolan just happened to know the local British M-I6 agent. "You know, I hear Montserrat is nice this time of year," Bolan called down the hatch.

Blancanales shrugged. "Montserrat it is."